# THE NOEWARE MAN

## WOVEN BRANCHES

A SOUTHERN SERIAL

## G. L YANCY

*For Dylan and Kristi*

# PRAISE FOR WOVEN BRANCHES
## BOOK 1, THE ROAD TO NOEWARE

★★★★★ G.L. Yancy is the next big thing
★★★★★ I Couldn't Put It Down
★★★★★ Incredible Author, Incredible Thrilling Read!
★★★★★ Nothing Beats Small Town Drama
★★★★★ Your Next Favorite Series
★★★★★ An "Oh My Gosh" Moment Around Every Corner
★★★★★ Soapy Goodness
★★★★★ Super Fun Read
★★★★★ Well, Butter My Backside and Call Me a Biscuit!!
★★★★★ Richly Developed Characters and A Surprise Around Every Corner
★★★★★ Fast-Paced Read Packed with Fun!
★★★★★ Excellent Series Debut
★★★★★ Wish I Could Give It More Stars
★★★★★ I LOVE THIS BOOK!
★★★★★ Exciting Read with Fascinating Characters!
★★★★★ It's A Wild Ride!
★★★★★ Wow! Just Wow!!
★★★★★ Take Me to Noeware, Please!

The Noeware Man
Copyright © 2024 by G.L. Yancy

Editing:
Cover Design by: AuthorTree
Interior Book Formatting: AuthorTree

All rights reserved under the International and Pan-American Copyright Conventions. No part of this book may be reproduced or transmitted in any form or by any means, electronic or mechanical, including photocopying, recording, or by any information storage and retrieval system, without permission in writing from the publisher.

This is a work of fiction. Names, places, characters and incidents are either the product of the author's imagination or are used fictitiously, and any resemblance to any actual persons, living or dead, organizations, events or locales is entirely coincidental.

Warning: the unauthorized reproduction or distribution of this copyrighted work is illegal. Criminal copyright infringement, including infringement without monetary gain, is investigated by the FBI and is punishable by up to 5 years in prison and a fine of $250,000.

# PROLOGUE
## 48 HOURS AFTER THE MURDER

He spent the night tossing and turning uncontrollably on the hay-padded pallet that acted as a makeshift bed on the floor of the uninsulated wooden shed. He shivered with full-body chills, caused not by the heavy morning dew collected on his filthy flannel blanket but by a level of anxiety higher than he had ever known. Two days and two nights, a full 48 hours, he had called this place home, though it had none of the comforts that home would provide. It would be dawn soon, he imagined, providing a natural light through the slats of the rickety, weather-worn walls. Natural light would be a welcome shift from the preternatural beams that shone streaks into this place all night—this horrible, wretched place. He wondered, not for the first time, how much longer he would be imprisoned in this solitary cell of his own making. With its cold, blue light—the ever-constant light—he imagined that this must be what it felt like to be tortured by a foreign adversary.

Wade Hansard had always been easily persuadable. As a child in grammar school, he was the "go-along" type, always willing to do what the cool kids did in hopes that a little of their popularity might rub off. At the behest of his classmates, he swallowed a baby frog on the playground in third grade just to receive a moment's attention, attention that would inevitably be awarded to Wilson Bass instead, a taller and more athletic black kid in his class. As soon as Wilson Bass had begun chanting, "Eat it! Eat it!" nobody cared what Wade was doing anymore. Wilson Bass, the bane of his existence. A handsome, fit darkie that never knew his place. Wade had thought that then and he thought it still.

In middle school, Wade had met and hung out with some guys from a rival elementary school that fed, along with his own school, into a single junior high. His new classmates, all Caucasian, introduced him to a new type of music. Bands with names like Oi, The Brotherhood, White Oasis were on regular rotation in his cassette player. That is until his mother heard them. She wasn't a fan of Wade's newfound friends, forbade him from listening to his new choice of music, and refused to allow him to shave his head like his chosen peers. She didn't understand him; she never understood him.

Alarmed at the concerning direction that she saw her son's life taking, Jerri Hansard, a single mother and psychotherapist in private practice, enrolled her son in a private school—the best private school that she could find in Columbus, Georgia. There, Wade was required to wear ironed khaki pants, a white button-down shirt, a belt, a tie, and brown leather shoes. Conformity was the highest law there, and Wade was required to wear its uniform. He despised that school.

Ironically, though it was lost on him, he only wanted to look and behave like his fellow anarchists. Jerri Hansard had suggested that her son try out for a sports team or join a club. She thought, anything to help the kid make healthy friends and "fit in". None of this was of interest to Wade; he no longer aspired to be popular. He had embraced his loner reputation—if he wanted nothing from anyone, no one could hurt him. All he wanted was to do his time, graduate, and get the hell out of Georgia. He had his sights set on rural Idaho or Oregon, someplace closer to the Northwest, a place better suited to enlightened people like him. People who understood the order of things, the hierarchy, the ones who wore the perceived crown of superiority—the master race.

Now, in the shed, the warm morning breeze brought in the familiar stench. Although he had grown accustomed to the smell over the past few days, he didn't notice it for the most part; each early morning had brought it anew, and he had to accustom himself to it afresh. It was unlike anything he had ever smelled before, like what one would imagine hell itself smelled like—sulfurous, scorched, and sweet. He forced himself to swallow the bile that was creeping up his throat and sat up, still covered with the blanket. He slapped the red UGA cap on his shaved head, muttering out loud, "Ha, you can't stop me from shaving my head now, can you, you dyke bitch?"

Wade was not Jerri Hansard's only child; in fact, he wasn't her child at all. He was fostered by Jerri as an infant when his birthmother died delivering him, a story that she never seemed comfortable telling. She always left the details vague—the details he always most wanted to hear. Jerri had a daughter of her own, Tina, who was seven years older than Wade and was born blind. Wade always suspected that his mother considered him a bad influence on her daughter, though he thought his mother, being an out lesbian, would have a worse effect. Gays weren't meant to have children, he thought, as they lived a perverted lifestyle unsuitable for properly mentoring kids. Freaks, queers were freaks, a scourge on humanity.

While Tina took dance classes and flute lessons with other children with visual disabilities, Wade rebelled against similar opportunities. Cub Scouts was for nerdy kids. Band was for geeks. Rather than socialize with his peers, Wade preferred to sit, isolated in his room, and create Dungeons and Dragons characters for games that he would never play. He was angry, and his hundreds of characters, built to be killing machines, gave him an outlet for his aggression. But at some point, it stopped being enough. But he didn't know how else to channel it, not for a long time.

Though Wade never considered her an attentive parent, Jerri was on the scene in what seemed like minutes the day in eleventh-grade Physical Education class that Wade had cornered and pinned down Tomas Garcia, a Hispanic classmate who wouldn't give him the basketball he was after. There were no fewer than a dozen basketballs available to the students, but Wade had his sights set on the one Tomas had chosen. This led to harsh words, shoving, a few thrown fists, and finally, a wooden broom handle being forcibly pressed against the Hispanic boy's throat while he lay gasping for air on the highly polished gym floor, Wade Hansard straddling the kid from above to prevent his escape. The other teens, some gasping, some cheering, were in a frenzy of adrenaline as they watched, but all Wade could hear was the blood in his ears and the echoing squeak of his sneakers on the gym floor as he leveraged ever-increasing pressure on his makeshift weapon.

Wade was expelled from school that day without protest from Jerri. She grew increasingly worried about her son's increasingly uncontrolled anger and started casting about for ways to help him manage it. She enrolled the teen in a "boot camp" for troubled kids, not having any other idea how to handle the hostility boiling up in her son, nor having any idea what the origin of his angst was, to begin with. He was there for six weeks, returned home to Columbus, stayed another 11 months, and on his eighteenth birthday, he packed a bag and left—Jerri silently looking on. Jerri only had occasional contact with her son from that day on, the occasions being whenever he was desperate for money—she was always good at that.

Money had been a constant issue for Wade Hansard. Columbus, Georgia, certainly wasn't Atlanta, but in some ways, it could be seen as a miniature version of the southern metropolis. The side streets of downtown were crawling with suburbanites cruising for illicit drugs and sketchy sex. It wasn't long before Wade decided that taking cash for favors from men of better means was an easy way to supplement the relatively low wages he made during the day as a laborer on various construction sites. He wasn't gay, but as long as he was receiving pleasure and not playing an active role in giving it, he could just about justify his part in the acts. If queers must exist, then he could use them for his benefit, or at least that was his reasoning.

His plan to get to Idaho—and the community of like-minded people he knew to be there, the kind of people he could count on to not look down on him—had been slow to start. He had thought about just starting out in that direction. He could walk and hitchhike and sleep wherever he found a place. But his tolerance for physical discomfort was not as great as his anarchist dreams, as he was learning all too vividly right now. He was willing to do this for a day or two if it got him enough money.

In the shed, he was becoming conditioned to the rancid smell, but the inevitable flies had just arrived. What seemed like hundreds of large flies, some people called them horseflies, descended on his hiding spot every morning. Landing on every exposed surface of his skin, he'd spend the day swiping them off, battling to keep them away from him—to no avail. His arms and face were covered in pink-tinged welts left from the bites of the insects. It was enough to drive a person mad.

*Wooooooooot*

In the distance, the train whistle. Always in this town, that damned train whistle. It was incessant. That type of sound had always set him on edge; now, it was the sound of a mournful conscience … if he had one. His nerves were frayed as it was; he just wanted to get paid and get out. Where the hell was the guy with his money, anyway? He'd wait another hour or so, then text him using the encrypted chat app that they had agreed to use to communicate, that is, if there was still any charge on the phone he had been given. He couldn't wait to leave this town behind him. Next stop, Utah. He'd done research on an Arian training camp up there. A group of like-minded men preparing for the coming race war. His people—finally.

around town, hoping to get a comment from her regarding the murder of her partner, Jessica Walters. A murder that had just taken place two days ago.

Allison approached the chrome-lined counter and sat on a red vinyl stool, trying to understand why her friend, Billy Washington, was shaking his head so vigorously at her. She glanced at the stool to her left and made her first eye contact with the husband of her partner, a husband that she was unaware existed until about an hour after Jessica's murder. "Well," Allison said to Dennis Hernandez with a heavy sigh, "I suppose this was inevitable."

Mayor's Office, Noeware, Ga.

"JERRI, THIS IS RUTH—AGAIN!" MAYOR RUTH BLAKELY, known to most of Tennyson County by her nickname, Ruthless, said into the voicemail of Jerri Hansard as if the vehemence of her tone could compel Jerri to answer. This was the third such voicemail that the mayor had left for her old friend over the past hour. All had been unreturned. Ruth's patience was wearing thin, if not necessarily with her friend, Jerri, then with life, in its current state, in general, which was trying her last nerve. Jerri was in the unfortunate position of being one of the few people who might be able to help Ruth maneuver the present state of things into something Ruth could control—and, therefore, tolerate.

Ruth Blakely ended the call and immediately placed

leave Washington and head back to Tennyson County, Georgia, ready or not—and soon.

### The Middle of Noeware Diner, Noeware, Ga.

"Billy, I told you a Monday morning rush was going to be too much for you with broken ribs; go sit down; I can manage," Ned Wilson, diner owner, said to his lone employee, Billy Washington. Billy had been the victim of an assault with a baseball bat just a few nights before but had been insistent that he could get back to work.

"Ned, I told you that these ribs are fractured, not broken. There is not a reason on this earth why I can't be here flinging eggs and bacon. You act like I jackhammer for a living."

"You do know that fractures are breaks, right?"

"If that is so, Dr. Wilson," Billy replied, teasing the older man, "then why are they spelled differently, huh? Not to mention, you've dropped that spatula twice already this morning; you need someone young and virile to help you around here."

Ned shook his head at Billy, watching the man flinch with every plate that he lifted, "I don't think that sentence means what you think it does." He looked up as the bell on the diner's front door chimed.

"I said take your cameras and tape recorders somewhere else and leave my customers in peace," Ned yelled at the reporters who were following Allison Edwards' every step

Georgetown, Washington D.C.

"Good morning, Claire," Camille Tennyson said by way of greeting her sister-in-law on her cell phone. She sat in her Tiffany blue bathrobe, staring at a breakfast of orange juice, coffee, and a sesame bagel, but she hadn't taken a single bite. After listening to Claire Montgomery rant anxiously for a few minutes, Camille interjected, "We have been over this numerous times, Claire; we'll change the trajectory of the headlines by moving up the campaign announcement. The press is already all over town trying to get the scoop on the murder; let's take advantage of their presence and show them how we handle a crisis." Camille's patience was running very short with Claire, who was not even close to the top of her list of favorite people. In fact, Claire Montgomery might just be Camille's least favorite person. She didn't care for anyone who rivaled her influence with her husband, Harrison—and as Harrison's sister, Claire had far too much for Camille's liking.

However, Camille was forced to deal with Claire for the moment, as Harrison Tennyson had chosen his sister to be the campaign manager for his soon-to-be-announced U.S. Senate bid, against Camille's attempted persuasion to instead use a hired gun from D.C. "We can use both the assault on Billy Washington and the murder of that Jessica person to our advantage. We'll work a 'law and order' message into the announcement speech." Camille gave a deep sigh as Claire continued to give her opinion on everything campaign-related, but she was thinking only one thing: she was going to have to

First the smell, then the flies, now the squeals. He could hear the rusted metal gate slam shut as the squeals grew louder. He tensed as the sound of muck boots sloshing through wet ground came ever closer. The shed door opened with a creak, allowing enough light in to make him squint his eyes. Though he should have been used to bright light, there were enough security lights illuminating this place overnight to keep Georgia Power in business. Refocusing, he saw that the darkie who owned the place had brought him breakfast, grits again, and a—newspaper?

"What the fuck is that?" Wade asked the man as he took it from his hand.

"It's a newspaper, boy. I reckon I'd not be surprised if it's the first one you've ever seen, ignorant fool."

"Watch it—"

"Look," the black man said without allowing Wade another word, "If I weren't being paid a handsome sum to hide you out, I'd take that broken pitchfork over there and kill you myself, you son of a bitch. I just thought you'd wanna see that you're famous."

"Famous? What the hell are you talking about?" Wade unfolded the newspaper and stared at the screaming bold headline, "BEWARE ... THE NOEWARE MAN."

The old man laughed as he opened the shed door with a creak. Uncle J.B. had a lot to do today, and he couldn't be distracted by some two-bit racist punk with a death wish. He had several dozen hungry hogs to feed.

MEANWHILE ...

another one to the Noeware Journal, where her brother-in-law, Carl Washington, was editor-in-chief. Carl answered the call on the first ring, "Ruthie—"

"Don't you 'Ruthie' me, Carl Washington! NOEWARE MAN? Seriously? That's too cute by half, Carl. I am not amused. Not to mention, you are absolutely sensationalizing the transgender aspect of this story. What are you thinking?"

"What I am thinking, Ruthie, is that today's edition has already sold four times the number of copies that a normal Monday paper would sell. I have a responsibility—"

"Don't talk to me about responsibility, you old fool. May I remind you that your own son, William, works part-time as a female impersonator and CAN READ? Your family, Carl, what about your responsibility to your family? You run a respectable paper; remember that. Lately, it is reading more like tabloid trash."

"I see where you're coming from, Ruth, but I can't say as I completely understand why you are taking this so personally."

"Tread lightly, Carl, final warning," Ruth said before ending the call and immediately answering the new one that was incoming.

"Chief Ernie Thomas, please tell me you have our suspect in custody," the mayor said into the phone, addressing Noeware's chief of police.

"Not yet, Ruth, I actually called to let you know about last night's sting."

"Sting? As in sting operation? What exactly are you talking about, Ernie?"

The mayor had been so focused on this morning's lead

front page headline, that she had neglected to look under the fold. Now, she took that opportunity.

"ERNIE THOMAS, WHAT IN THE HELL?" She yelled, feeling as if her head was about to explode.

"Ruth, you said that you wanted something to change the headlines."

"So, you thought you'd perform a sting operation, using public funds—WITHOUT, I MIGHT MENTION, INFORMING YOUR MAYOR—and throw a bunch of men cruising an alley for a quick blowjob into a jail cell?"

"Well, it made the front page, but I thought I would call and warn you—"

"Warn me about what, pray tell?"

"One of the men that we arrested—"

"Spit it out, Ernie, I am short an assistant today, and you are depleting every last ounce of my patience."

"Dr. Don Givens," Ernie Thomas said.

"What about him? Oh, dear God! Ernie, are you telling me that Dr. Givens was arrested in the sting? Commissioner Harrison Tennyson's son-in-law? THAT Dr. Don Givens?"

"I'm afraid so, Ruth."

Mayor Ruth Blakely ended the call without another word, sat back in her chair, sighed loudly, and said, "What else could possibly go wrong this morning?"

As if on cue, there was a soft knock on the already-opened door of the office. Ruth, though she was afraid to look, glanced in that direction.

"Ruth? It's me, Misti Waddell. You know, Cash's wife?"

Just shoot me, Ruth thought to herself as she stared back at the rail-thin woman with stringy blond hair, a barely there mini-skirt, impossibly high heels, and a grayish complexion.

"Well, you've picked the worst possible day to return to town, Ms. Waddell. You've been out of sight for so long, not to mention out of mind, I assumed you were dead. Now, I can see that you are only halfway there."

Nadine's Boarding House, Tennyson County, Ga.

NADINE BASSETTE HAD BEEN OPERATING HER "BOARDING house" in Tennyson County for decades. She had been discreetly approached in the late 1970s by a member of the county commission and offered a proposition. She would be allowed to run a business, without the need to look over her shoulder, that would fill a niche in the community, and the commission would make sure that she had a monopoly within the profession that she worked—the world's oldest. Nadine accepted the opportunity, converted the family home that she had grown up in into a stately "inn," and brought some attractive young ladies into her employ.

Nadine, with her voluptuous figure, flawless cream-colored skin, light pink bouffant hairstyle, oversized bosom, and frank manner, ran a very classy establishment. That is, as classy as a house of ill repute could be. She put up with zero drama and assumed the role of house mother, often referred to as madam, with zeal. The women who worked for her were clean, educated, healthy, and well-spoken. In fact, they were the finest "ladies of the evening" in South Georgia, and Nadine would accept nothing less. Customers came from far and wide, knowing they could trust Nadine with their needs, health, and reputations.

This Monday morning, as she stood at the front desk looking over her books, her white poodle, Rufus, by her side, Nadine glanced up to see the front door open. Jeremiah Waddell, the embodiment of Tennyson County shame, entered cautiously. He came to a stop just a step or two inside the front door. Making eye contact with Nadine, he opened his mouth to speak but was quickly interrupted.

"Stop right there, Jeremiah Waddell. Do not come another step closer to this desk. I told you years ago, when you lost your right hand, that you had better become proficient with your left one because you were not welcome here around any of my girls. It's still early in the day, and Phenix City is only about an hour and a half away. There are whores-a-plenty there. If you leave now, you can get your business done and be home by lunchtime. We've all heard it doesn't take you long—to do your business," the madam said, surveying the man from top to bottom as she adjusted her more than generous cleavage.

"Calm yourself, Nadine, I ain't here for nothin' like that." He swallowed, then continued, "I just wanted to know if you got some work going."

"Well, in that case, the answer is HELL NO! You are even less likely to get a job here than you are a quickie. Don't let the door hit ya, Hun." Nadine returned her attention to her books as Rufus yawned, walked in a small circle, and plopped onto his overstuffed red-flannel bed.

Seconds after Jeremiah Waddell exited the boarding house, the sound of wobbling furniture could be heard from the hallway as a very intoxicated Harrison Tennyson, head of the county commission, made his way to the lobby. He was fumbling with every step and holding on to the walls and tables for support.

"Harry, I am going to call Hank and have him give you a ride home, you've been trashed all night," Nadine said. She was referring to the closest thing that Tennyson County, Georgia had to a taxi service, Hank Johnson and his army green pickup truck.

"I am not going home. I am going to city hall."

"Well, I think that's not one of your better ideas, Einstein," the madame replied, head shaking.

Nadine had barely finished her sentence when Harrison shut the front door behind him, using the doorknob for stability, car keys in hand.

Picking up the phone, Nadine dialed a familiar number, and the call was answered after two rings.

"Ruthie, it's Nadine, Sugar, I'm afraid Harry Tennyson is on his way to see you, and he's drunker than Cooter Brown."

# PART ONE

**The Day Before the Campaign Announcement**

# CHAPTER 1
# THE GRAND HOTEL, NOEWARE, GA

Claire Montgomery, general manager of the Grand Hotel, was sitting at her computer, pretending to get some work done. The good news was all available rooms were full of paying guests. The bad news was that those guests were almost exclusively members of the press. The truth was she was unable to concentrate on anything work-related. It seemed that within the past 48 hours, her entire world had collapsed. Her hotel was on partial lockdown due to a murder on the fourth floor, which was now crawling with FBI agents. The murderer had yet to be apprehended, and she had been interviewed until she had nearly lost her voice—by both detectives and the press. Claire never bought into the adage that any press was good press. She didn't need her hotel to be known as "murder central" in Tennyson County. Neither did she need the new hotel owners—she had been informed just this morning that the current owner had accepted an offer of purchase from an LLC, though she had no way of knowing how long such a deal had been under consideration—to have this be their first impression of her as manager. Oh well, Claire thought to herself, I'll be running a senate campaign soon enough, anyway.

In addition to her place of employment being an active crime scene, her brother was on an absolute drunken tear. She knew why, even if no one else did. He had confided to her only a year ago that he had an interracial adult daughter, born out of wedlock, who just happened to be transgender. He claimed, at the time, to have just found out about her, though Claire was highly dubious about that. In the deep South, even in the year of our lord 2024, a politician could lose votes over such illicit information. Some might even suspect that such a man would want to sweep the existence of such an indiscretion under the rug—maybe six feet under it.

Claire herself knew just how impossible it could be to imagine her brother doing something like committing murder, not necessarily because of his strong conscience, but at least because of his weak stomach. Harrison Tennyson had never been the strong one in the family—she had had to play that role after the mysterious disappearance of their older sister, Olivia. Emotionally, Harrison could still be childlike, and her protection of him was as habitual to him as it was to her. Protecting her brother had basically been her life's mission.

Now, in addition to those two unsettling situations, Claire was preparing to deal with the impending return of her sister-in-law, Camille Tennyson. Camille had started as a spoiled brat and only got worse with age. Claire could handle the woman most of the time because she was almost never home. Camille had spent the better part of the last few years traveling extensively to test the waters for and raise money on behalf of Harrison's upcoming senate run. Claire shook her head, thinking about the last time she and Camille had been in the same room together. Oil and water, that's what they were. Or maybe phosphorus and air—liable to ignite with the smallest friction. Their argument that day, over Harrison having asked Claire to assume the role of his campaign manager, had nearly brought the women to blows. No, Claire was certainly not looking forward to Camille's plane touching back down in Georgia.

As if all of that weren't enough, Claire had blown out the hotel's marketing budget on promotional items to be used for Founders' Day, only to have Mayor Ruth Blakely cancel the weekend's festivities altogether. Only twice in the city's history had Founders' Day weekend been canceled—this weekend and back in the early 1970s, when Claire and Harrison's sister, Olivia, had gone missing. The Tennyson family had been left devastated by the disappearance, and Harrison and Claire's entire futures had changed in an instant.

Each of these pressures would have been significant on their own; now, they were converging into a single weight on Claire. She wasn't sure she could handle one more thing, such that when she opened the paper to see that her niece's husband had been arrested the previous evening for public indecency, Claire almost started to laugh. But any hysterical mirth she might have felt quickly turned as she realized that she wasn't the only one in the lobby holding a copy of today's paper. No, in fact, the paper had practically sold out, prompting an unheard-of second printing at just 8:00 a.m. Everyone was keen for news on the murdered girl, but the sting had been an extra bombshell. Dr. Don Givens was a gifted cardiac surgeon at the local hospital—which just happened to be named after the Tennyson family following a sizeable endowment over 40 years ago that was still earning interest. His was among the names of the individuals caught soliciting sex in a seedy alley behind a nightclub located in a part of town that no Tennyson would ever be seen in. That was Claire's last straw. She headed into her office to escape the whispers and stares that were starting to reach a fever pitch. She wasn't sure that she would leave her office until dark.

"Damn it," Claire said out loud, "I forgot to call Congressman McDonald." Congressman Steve McDonald had had a brief affair with Camille a few years ago. An end was put to the fling when Harrison found out, though his reaction had perhaps not been as volcanic as one might expect of a man who learned his wife was cheating. The congressman had been so worried about retribution for the infidelity that he had quickly agreed to endorse Harrison to be Georgia's next senator. Everything had been squared away, or at least that is what all parties thought. Recently, the congressman had been calling Harrison repeatedly, even though Harrison had made it clear to the man that anything campaign-related was to go through Camille.

Claire picked up her phone and dialed the congressman's number. Taking a large earring off her right ear in order to place the phone against it, she waited while ring after ring went unanswered. Finally, a voicemail greeting played, and at the tone, Claire began to speak. "Steve, this is Claire Montgomery. Harrison told me that you have been trying to reach him. You have been told repeatedly that anything political should be addressed to Camille. Let's be honest; we both know that you know how to reach her. Do not call Harry again. There is no reason for the two of you to have words. I'll let Camille know to expect your call." Claire ended the call and went back to pretending to concentrate on work.

Outside Claire's office, Daisy Wei was currently working alone at the front desk. Daisy was having a hard time with her computer, as always. Glancing up from the screen, she noticed Cash Waddell, the town hoodlum (and the secret object of Daisy's desire), walk into the lobby. Daisy thought it was strange to see Cash at the hotel a few days ago; for him to return now was downright bizarre. Something was up, she decided, and she was pretty sure that she knew what it was. He had finally noticed her, too, she thought, and he was looking for reasons to stop by and see her. With this realization, Daisy smiled and blushed. Maybe she'd even work up the moxy to ask him out for a coffee date, blissfully heedless of the fact that he'd be as incongruous in The Mean Bean as in the Grand Hotel.

"Daisy, I need to speak to Claire," Cash said, looking sternly into her right eye, the left eye covered with a black patch. His black mullet was mussed and his clothes disheveled, as if he hadn't yet gone to bed. He had a look on his face that was a blend of worry and determination. Daisy, whether shy or coy or both, avoided Cash's direct gaze, keeping her eyes on her computer. "Did you hear me?" Cash asked again, louder and more slowly than the first time. He had little patience for the young Asian woman—she struck him as flighty, which wasn't far off the mark.

"I'm sorry, I was a little preoccupied by this ... computer.

I'm afraid that Claire is in her office and has given me strict instructions not to interrupt her for any reason."

Daisy had scarcely finished the sentence before Cash had walked around the front desk and into the general manager's office—without a knock.

"Are you insane?" Claire asked Cash without any further greeting.

"I am not playing with you, Claire. You haven't returned any of my calls. We have a lot of business to discuss."

"Keep your voice down, you idiot. I'll call you in about an hour. Until then, I do not want to see you within two blocks of this hotel. Do I make myself clear?"

## CHAPTER 2
## MAYOR'S OFFICE, NOEWARE, GA

"Well, you might as well have a seat," Mayor Ruth Blakely said as she used her walker to lift herself to a standing position behind her desk. Making her way towards the door between her office and the waiting area, she glanced over her shoulder and addressed Misti Waddell, "I'm afraid that my assistant, Tina, is off for a few days. May I offer you anything? Coffee? Tea? Penicillin?"

"I guess I deserve that, seein' how I look and all, but I am clean, Ruth. I've been clean for a while now—the clinic says so." Misti avoided direct eye contact with the mayor, displaying a level of significant shame for her current state of disarray.

Ruth's dark complexion turned ashen, and she suddenly regretted her offer for the young woman to sit in her finely upholstered chair. She raised an eyebrow over the frame of her thick eyeglasses, "Why exactly are you here, Misti?" her voice softening the slightest bit.

"Well, I want custody of my little girl," Misti Waddell replied.

"I see. But why are you HERE?" Ruth asked again.

"I need your help."

Ruth sighed, "I have a lot going on, Misti, too much, actually. I couldn't possibly help you right now, even if I were inclined to do so to begin with."

"I know that you hate the Waddell family, I get that, but I am not one of them anymore, Ruth, I never really was. The only thing I want is to get Annie out of that house. I don't think it is safe for her there. She's an innocent little girl, Ruth."

With a roll of her eyes, Ruth sat on the corner of her desk and looked directly at Misti Waddell, "I suppose you think that she is safer living rough with you?"

"I ain't homeless, Ruth. I got me a room and everything," Misti said proudly, her posture improving.

"A room? You expect to raise a child in a single room?"

"Well, it's a start, ain't it? They are raisin' her in not much more than a room in that house, too. I know that my little girl is better off with me than she is with those animals."

"I won't argue with you there. However, I don't think any court of law is going to look very kindly on how you live your life, Misti."

Misti sat up straight in her chair and proudly professed, "I'm a new woman, Ruth. I've given my life to the lord."

Shaking her head, Ruth replied, "That's all well and good, Misti, but the court is going to want more than that. It's admirable that you've given your life to Jesus; the problem is, you've sold the rest of yourself to every man within a thirty-mile radius of Tennyson County."

"Look," Misti replied exasperated, "I know that you can't relate personally, but if you did have a child of your own, and you had a chance to save her life, wouldn't you do anything in your power to do just that?"

Ruth felt as if she had just been slapped barehanded. She recovered herself quickly, too quickly for someone like Misti—preoccupied with herself as she was—to notice.

Ruth had barely had time to usher Misti Waddell out of her office before Harrison Tennyson arrived. As Nadine Bassette had promised, he was more intoxicated than Ruth had ever seen him, and that was saying something.

"Well, I was wondering when you'd show up," the mayor said contemptuously. "You have a lot of damn nerve stumbling in here like a common wino, smelling of expensive scotch and cheap women."

With tears in his eyes, Harrison replied, "He was our child, Ruthie, our child."

"SHE was never our child, Harrison; she belonged to the Walters—always did."

"That's not what I meant, and you know it."

"I know that I never should have told you in the first place. I knew one day you'd behave like this."

"Like what, Ruth? What am I behaving like? Like a father in mourning for his son? A son that I never had the chance to meet?"

Losing the last of her patience, Ruth replied, "YOU NEVER HAD A SON, HARRY! YOU HAD A DAUGHTER. She was your FIRST daughter. Why can't you say it?"

Falling into the chair recently vacated by Misti Waddell, Harrison Tennyson rubbed the scar on his forehead. "I don't understand it," was all he could offer. Exhaling into a resigned sigh, Ruth replied, "I don't necessarily understand it either, Harry, but it's not mine to understand."

With that, Harrison Tennyson broke down into uncontrollable sobs. Placing his face into both open hands, he wept. Finally catching his breath, Harry said, "You kept this from me. I wouldn't have even known about the child! You were never going to tell me, even after all these years? I wouldn't have known if that insane mother of yours had not gotten wind of the senate run and tried to blackmail Camille."

"We've been over this, Harry, and I am too busy to rehash it today. I didn't tell you about Jessica because there was no need to. You made me promise when we were kids that I would leave Tennyson County and make something of myself. That is exactly what I did."

"Then you came back. Why in the hell did you come back?"

"That's a topic for another day, Harrison Tennyson. I do not have time to explain that to you—not now. Now, you are going to leave your car, wherever it is, and I am going to have Hank drive you back to Tennyson Place," Ruth said as she picked up the phone to dial Hank's number.

"But I—"

"Nope, not another word. I'll call Hank, and you and I will continue this conversation later—much later."

"Tonight, when I come over—"

"Ohhh no, you are not coming over tonight. Nor any other night, not for quite some time."

"But—"

"But nothing."

"Ruth, you need me."

With a look as hot as an incinerator, Ruth Blakely looked Harrison Tennyson squarely in the eyes.

"Need? NEED you? The back massager in the top drawer of my nightstand begs to differ, Harry, and I will tell you another damn thing, I trust its three-year-old generic batteries that I purchased at the dollar store on clearance more than I trust you or any member of your whole rotten family right now."

Harrison Tennyson was stunned—lost. He displayed the look of a man who was only then learning that he had nowhere to turn, not a friend in the world. The expression that he returned to Ruth was pleading, desperate, and hopeless. Through tears, he responded, "Please don't pretend that sex is all we have, Ruthie."

"Harry Tennyson, get yourself a cup of coffee or three and get out of my office. This grieving father routine is not a good look for you, and it just might give the FBI pause. I have important things to do, and dealing with you is not in the top 10 pertinent items on that list. I'll call Hank, you wait out front on the bench so I don't have to smell you."

# CHAPTER 3
# MIDDLE OF NOEWARE DINER, NOEWARE, GA

Billy Washington gave Gail Wilson the total for her takeout breakfast as her ex-husband, Ned Wilson, stood by his side. Gail and Ned looked at each other, almost rendering Billy invisible. Receiving her change and a white plastic bag covered in red pre-printed "Thank you" messages, Gail addressed Ned, "Founders' Day festivities canceled; I bet your daddy is turning in his grave."

"That man loved Founders' Day for sure," Ned replied, "but I suppose Ruth had to make a difficult decision. I mean, there is a killer on the loose. Was she expected to have a town-wide celebration before he is caught?" He wiped his hands anxiously on his apron, never breaking eye contact with Gail.

"She made the right decision for sure; it's just a shame. This town could have used a little pick-me-up right about now."

Just then, Gail's sister, Dr. Meg Givens, walked up from

behind and tapped the blonde woman on the shoulder, causing Gail to nearly drench them both in hot coffee.

"Meg, you damn near scared the life out of me." Noticing her sister's wig immediately, Gail asked, "I see you've gone as blonde as me today. Are you in disguise, or have you just decided to have more fun?"

"Let's grab a corner booth and talk for a bit. I'll call Aunt Claire and let her know that you'll be a little late arriving at the hotel for your shift. God knows she'll understand that there's a lot going on."

On the way to a booth, both women nodded at Allison Edwards, who was sitting across a Formica table from Dennis Hernandez, the husband of her recently murdered partner. His hair was dark brown, about the same color as his eyes, and unkempt. He had a light olive complexion, but it looked sallow at the moment—who knew how long it had been since the man slept? The corduroy blazer he wore had leather elbow patches that might have been fashionable twenty years ago; at present, it was crumpled in the way that a blazer only gets after several hours of car rides or being shoved unfolded into a duffle bag. His shoes were brown leather oxfords; one had untied laces. His facial expression was one of complete bewilderment.

"I have to admit, I am a little nervous talking to you," Dennis said finally after a long, awkward silence.

"I can't imagine why," Allison replied, "you are only the husband of my life partner. A husband, who until a few days ago, I was completely unaware said life-partner had. Happens all the time, right?"

"I didn't—"

"Nope. Stop," Allison interrupted. "You do not get to talk until I ask a few questions, and I sure have a few."

"Fair enough, I'll do the best I can to answer them all," Dennis Hernandez replied, settling in nervously. Dennis seemed to understand that he would get nowhere protesting, as Allison was determined to play the detective role in this interrogation.

"I don't even know where to start," Allison said, still in a state of disbelief over the entire situation. "Okay, here's one; how long have you been, um, were you married to Jess?"

His eyes glistened with moisture as he looked toward Allison, though he avoided direct eye contact, "We were married for almost five years. We met in a park outside of the CDC building, I would often take my lunch there to get out of the house on nice days. I work from home, teaching online classes for the university. We were so happy—"

"STOP!" Allison exclaimed. "You don't get to talk yet, and I'd ask you, at a time like this, to focus on facts and not your marital bliss, or I might not be able to prevent myself from hurdling this table and throttling you."

"Look, I can only imagine how angry you are, and you have every right to be angry, but I hope you will let me explain."

Allison paused. She was angry—much angrier than Dennis was, it seemed. Why wasn't he angry, now that she thought about it? She sighed loudly, slumped back in the booth, crossed her arms and said, "Alright, spill."

"I was aware of your relationship with Jessica," Dennis said. At this, Allison slammed her mug down on the table, belatedly grateful that she'd already drunk most of it and Billy had not been back with a refill. This, of course, explained why Dennis wasn't slamming mugs around himself. She started to speak, but Dennis quickly continued, raising his palms to her in a gesture of mercy, "WHILE being unaware of the extent of it. I understood from day one of our relationship that she was bisexual, and I knew that she had other encounters."

"Encounters? ENCOUNTERS? Are you kidding me right now? Jess and I shared a life together. Encounters?"

"With all due respect, Allison, and I really do mean this respectfully, you only saw my wife on the weekends in Atlanta. Her actual life took place in Indiana during the week."

Allison paused, absorbing what he had said. She took one deep breath and exhaled; when she continued, her voice was quieter but with venom creeping in.

"Are you suggesting that what Jess and I had was just an every weekend tryst? An affair?"

"Well, when you say it that way, it sounds a little more harsh than I intended—"

Before Dennis Hernandez could finish his reply, he was wearing what was left of the lukewarm coffee that Allison Edwards had in her mug. The look of shock he wore on his face matched the expression of every other person in the diner at that moment, a group of people who were doing their very best to eavesdrop on the most anticipated confrontation in Noeware, Georgia, since a drunken Gail Wilson strolled in years ago demanding a divorce from her husband, Ned.

Without another word, Dennis wiped his face with a napkin, dabbed halfheartedly at the liquid soiling his jacket, and stood from the booth. "I think it's probably a good idea for us to finish this conversation later." With those parting words, he headed for the exit door.

Rushing over to the booth, bar towels in hand, Billy Washington started to wipe the booth and table.

"Billy, I am so sorry for the mess, let me get that," Allison said while grabbing white paper napkins from a table-top dispenser. Her face was beet-red with a combination of embarrassment and rage.

"Nooooo, G.H., I got this here mess. This is the most drama we've had in here all year, and I am here for it. It reminds me of that time on Search for Tomorrow, you know when Travis and Liza—"

"Billy, not right now, please."

"Not another word, G.H., and I'll bring you a fresh cup of coffee."

A blond woman in the next booth, as if somehow completely oblivious to the current happenings, said to Billy, "Excuse me, I don't think it is my glass of sweet tea."

Glancing back at the woman with surprise, Billy replied, "Well, then whose tea is it, Girl, Honey? We have a situation going on here."

Billy Washington turned to head back to the counter but ran abruptly into Chief Ernie Thomas, Noeware, Georgia's head law enforcement officer and recently inaugurated nemesis of Allison Edwards.

"Well, pardon me, chief, I didn't mean to get all up in your grill while heading to the grill," Billy said, laughing off the situation.

"No problem, Billy, I just came over to make sure that our

visitor from Atlanta was doing okay," Ernie said while grinning and looking at Allison.

"When and if I need your help, Chief Thomas, I will call 9-1-1. Until then, I would kindly ask you to mind your own business," Allison responded just before storming out of the diner and directly into a group of reporters. Walking briskly through them, in hopes of avoiding a barrage of questions that she did not currently have answers to, she stepped off the curb without looking and into the street.

Brakes squealed for a good five feet, leaving black skid marks on the asphalt as a pink vintage Cadillac convertible came to a stop.

"Hey, watch where you're going, girl. Imogene here about plowed you down," said a startled woman with hair like cotton candy and a chest like a basket of melons.

"Imogene?" Allison responded awkwardly, a bit in shock from the close call and not knowing what else to say.

"Oh yeah, my pride and joy. This caddy has seen me through the worst and best of times, but she about took all your cares away."

"Ha. Why do you think I didn't get out of the way?" Allison replied.

Grabbing a miniature white poodle from the passenger side of the car, the colorful woman said, "I'm Nadine Bassette, and you must be the girl writing the story for the paper."

"Allison Edwards," Allison acknowledged, not surprised that the woman already knew who she was. Due to a story in the local newspaper, everyone in this small town knew who Allison was.

"Nice to meet you, Allison, but my dog, Rufus, and I

would kindly ask you to look both ways before crossing the street. Imogene's tires were recently cleaned, and we don't need to get them all covered in dead Yankee." Nadine said as Rufus panted excitedly.

Filled with emotion, and finally unable to contain it, Allison burst into tears. The madam wrapped an arm around Allison in a motherly embrace and held her, ignoring the small line of traffic that was backing up behind them. Rufus allowed a low whimper.

Meanwhile, back inside the diner, sisters Gail Wilson and Dr. Meg Givens talked in their corner booth, both still startled by the recent exchange between Allison Edwards and Dennis Hernandez.

"See," Meg said, "you and I could have been on the receiving end of that cup of joe if Allison had any idea that we already knew about Jessica's husband. Now, don't you agree that I was right about us keeping that from her? It was awkward enough having to admit to her that we hired a private investigator to research her life; it wasn't our place to ruin it, too."

"I suppose you were right. I just feel bad about the whole thing. I haven't even had time to offer her my condolences," Gail replied.

Meg shook her head and smiled, "I think your condolences were assumed when you were the person to tell her about Jessica's murder, to begin with."

"Maybe you're right. May we change the subject?"

"Please," a relieved Meg replied.

"So, why the blonde wig," Gail asked her sister.

"My hair is coming out in clumps, the alopecia is flaring

up, and I suppose it does help throw the press off a little," Meg replied while smoothing down her hair.

"Well, you look like absolute hell. And what alopecia? This is the first I have heard about it. When's the last time you ate?"

"I had a slice of leftover pizza last night, I'll be okay."

"No, you won't. You'll eat half of this biscuit that I just got, and you'll tell me how you are," Gail demanded as she unwrapped her breakfast.

"If you mean, how am I feeling about my husband being arrested in a vice operation while he was cruising for sex with other men, I'm just peachy, thanks for asking," Meg said sarcastically.

"I can't imagine what you must be feeling right now."

"Of course, you can't. You are in love with the perfect man, who happens to love you even more, but you are too stubborn to enjoy your happily ever after."

"This conversation isn't about me and Ned, Meg; it's about your feelings about Don's situation."

"I know," Meg sighed in exasperation, "and I am sorry for being testy. It's just, I have no idea how to feel about this situation." While speaking to her sister, Meg noticed a new arrival at the counter of the diner. Without saying another word, she stood and walked over to the familiar woman.

"Dr. Hansard?" Meg asked, though she already knew for sure who she was addressing. The woman had been her husband's therapist for almost two years.

Turning away from Billy Washington, who was taking her order, Dr. Jerri Hansard replied, "Meg, I was just grabbing a quick cup of coffee to go; I didn't expect to see anyone that I knew." By her tone, she didn't sound altogether happy about it either.

"I just wanted to say that I am sorry that you are caught up in all of this 'Noeware Man' mess. The paper did an entire expose in the Sunday edition once the police identified Wade as the suspect. I am afraid that the press will eagerly await a statement from you. And I am eagerly awaiting an explanation from you regarding my husband's recent behavior."

"I appreciate the word of warning about the article. And you know that I am unable to discuss your husband with you; what he and I discuss is confidential."

"I do know that, but I just don't understand—"

"Talk to your husband, Meg. I have a daughter who is in complete shock because her foster brother has assaulted a man and killed a woman. I have enough on my plate right now."

Clearing his throat, Billy Washington looked sternly at the spiked-haired brunette woman in front of him, "Ladies, there is a line forming behind you, and I am sure that Bruce here would like to get to the train depot. Would you like to step aside? Or, you can go ahead and give your order to the man that your foster son assaulted."

Red-faced, Jerri Hansard exited the diner without ordering and made her way straight to City Hall.

# CHAPTER 4
# MAYOR'S OFFICE, NOEWARE, GA

"Cora, I gave Tina some time off; what with all of this craziness going on, I don't have time to chat right now," Ruth Blakely said into her cellphone while sitting at a desk filled with stacks of papers.

"Quit fretting, Ruthie, I'm not planning on keeping you long. I am just letting you know that I am jarring the last of the tomatoes this afternoon, before I turn the beds over to collards, so you can stop by."

"Are you hearing me, Cora? I said—"

"I heard exactly what you said, big sister, and I ain't never asked you a question. I am jarring those tomatoes, and I will be seeing you here around three this afternoon."

Without waiting for a reply, Cora Washington ended the call.

The mayor sighed in resignation as she added a trip out to her sister's house to her growing mental list of *to-dos*. She glanced at her left wrist to check her watch, which was conspicuously missing. Looking up, she addressed a welcome face.

"Well, I suppose this is better than a return call," Ruth said to her old friend, Jerri Hansard.

"Rue, I don't even know what to say. The irony of this situation is hardly lost on me, I am just so incredibly sorry."

"How was the traffic coming from Columbus?"

"How was the traffic? You can play games with others, Rue Blakely, but your attempt at avoidance will get you nowhere with me. I am one of only a handful of people who can imagine what you are going through right now, and I am here for you when you are ready to talk."

"As much as I appreciate the gesture, Jerri, I think your daughter, Tina, needs you much more than I do right now, but I would sure appreciate you meeting me over on this side of the desk before you go. I may not be ready to talk, but I could use a hug," Ruth said in a rare moment of vulnerability, tears forming in her eyes.

Jerri Hansard embraced her old friend. The two women had been the best of friends since their days as college roommates. They were each the other's closest confidante, the mutual holders of all secrets. Harrison Tennyson thought that Ruth Blakely needed him, but Jerri Hansard was the only person left on Earth that Ruth truly needed.

"I'm assuming that Tina is at her apartment?" Jerri asked while leaning back from Ruth. The mayor had quickly ended their embrace.

"Yes. I have spoken to her twice this morning. She is in shock, and who could blame her, but she is holding up well."

"I appreciate, as always, you taking care of my little girl, Rue."

"Your little girl isn't so little anymore, Jerri. How long do you think you'll be in town?"

"Certainly not very long; there are no hotel rooms available within miles of Tennyson County."

"I assumed you'd be staying at Tina's apartment."

"Oh, no, Tina does amazingly well with her visual impairment, but she has trouble when others are occupying her personal space. She has every inch of that little apartment committed to memory, so another person moving around forces her to question every step, especially when she is under a lot of stress."

"Then you'll stay with me at the condo, and I won't take no for an answer. Stay as long as you want. It'll be like old times."

"Like old times?" Jerri Hansard responded with a sly look. "So, a cheap bottle of wine and a joint next to the turntable?"

"Ha," Ruth laughed, "maybe not just like old times."

"I appreciate the offer. How about I plan to stay tonight, and we play it by ear after that?"

"Fair enough," the mayor responded as Jerri Hansard headed toward the door. She stopped and made a quick turn, "Willa—"

"She's fine, Jerri, just fine. I'll warn you, though, just in case you run into her, she's still carrying around that old picture of Tina."

Jerri sighed forcibly as she turned back toward the door, "That poor old soul. One wonders how a loving God could let a woman go through what Willa has gone through."

"That's how I keep my faith in God, Jerri; that old woman doesn't appear to remember any of it. That, my friend, is merciful."

With Jerri Hansard gone, Ruth sat back down behind her desk. The weight of the last few days was weighing on her like a 40 lb. sack of flour. While she would rather saw off her own arm with a rusty knife than do what she knew was right, she picked up her cellphone. She sent one text message to Chief Ernie Thomas, another to Allison Edwards, both with the same message: Meet me in my office this evening at six, it's very important.

# CHAPTER 5
# ATLANTA, GA., PIEDMONT AVE.,
1975

She could barely recall that her name was Wilhelmina Banks, and she had long since forgotten where she was from—though the phantom moan of a train whistle remained fixed in her psyche. It would appear in her memory, or perhaps her imagination—she didn't really know anymore—at odd times. It felt like a happy memory, if that's what it was, but it played on her nerves, sometimes repeating itself in unending echoes. Perhaps not in the moment, but in the hours following, she'd find herself wound as tight as the tension springs on the ancient John Deer baler she and her brother helped her dad with each summer, sharp grass stems cutting their arms and faces with a million tiny cuts as the burning sun slipped past the broken-down barn in a blaze of red.

Now, she paced a near trench in the burnt orange shag carpet of the motor lodge on Piedmont Avenue that she had called home for, well, God only knew how long. She was previously unfamiliar with areas such as this, where strip joints, gay bookstores, and bathhouses lined the seedy streets. Private lingerie modeling shows were advertised in neon lights on windowless brick buildings, and hookers and pimps worked every dimly lit corner. If it occurred to her to wonder what her younger self would have thought of her life now, she shook that thought away half-formed into the leftover cigarette smoke that lingered in her room from visitors past.

Her room was solitary and sparsely furnished. There was only a bed, a nightstand, a desk, a dusty fake plant in a macrame holder suspended from the corner ceiling, and a lamp to fill the otherwise empty space, a space as vacant and dismal as her mind and soul were becoming. There was a faded picture of a rural cabin on the wall, the paint on its cheap wooden frame chipped, like several of her teeth, the repercussion of attempts at refusing to participate in this ongoing hell. There was no phone, for obvious reasons, only the occasional palmetto bug climbing the wall for company. But there was a clock, an incessantly ticking faux wood wall clock with ugly brass fittings and a cheap paper face behind its glass. She could feel her sanity escape a bit with each aggravatingly monotonous tick, and she became even madder with the horrid responding tocks. Her life, or what was left of it, slipped away second by second.

Occasionally, she would stop pacing long enough to open the drawer of the nightstand beside her filthy bed and rub the front cover of the bible that resided there, compliments of the Gideons. Her prayer was always the same—for God to take her overnight in her sleep. Then she'd close the drawer, glance around the room with its dust-covered baseboards and its water-stained ceiling, and resign herself to her new reality.

Willa knew her prayers were silly, as she didn't sleep at night. No, the overnight hours were her worst hours. That's when they came—the men. Usually, they came one at a time, smelling of stale cigarettes and whiskey; sometimes, there were two. All of them treated her like a tattered possession, a thing that they had rented for an hour at a time. Which is what they had done. They'd come in, undress, undress her, or sometimes make her undress for them, climb on top of her, do their business, and leave. Her mouth, her vagina, her anus—orifices for orgasm, nothing more. She was no human to them, only part of their command. She began to think of herself as subhuman, too.

This same routine took place day in and day out, seven days a week, every single day. Wilhelmina had often protested in the beginning when she could still feel things. A Sunday off, anything to break up the parade of horrors. The reply from the "boss" was always the same, a closed-fisted pop across her face, but inside a pillow, so the bruising wouldn't be as bad. Not that any of the customers cared about a bruise. The pillow certainly didn't prevent the pain.

Pain. That was now her life. Physical pain when she protested, and physical pain when the "gentlemen" that rented her were too rough. Emotional pain, always. She missed the thought of her family back home, wherever that was. Most of the names had long since faded from memory; the faces were starting to follow. They were black cardboard cutouts labeled Ma and Pa, a taller one that was her brother. Another, impossibly small. The pills were wiping her reality away. The boss called them her *happy pills*. Wilhelmina had been fed the pills like candy, Satan's sweet treats. They were prescribed to others as a way of lessening seizures or anxiety. They were given to Wilhelmina to make her obedient and carefree. The pills just made her numb, and mostly, she was fine with that.

She'd once thought that escape was only as far away as the rental office of the motor lodge. She'd made a plan for just the right moment—sometime around 8:00 in the morning when the boss was drunk or already passed out, maybe he'd forget to lock the door. The grim reality set in when she saw the boss laughing and smoking with the manager one afternoon. It seemed he was happy to look the other way as long as his rooms stayed rented and maybe some extra money rolled in on the side. Call it a tip. No, there was no escape from the smell of mildew and stale sex that lingered in the air of the room, as if the wood-paneled walls themselves created the aromatic blend of sin and evil.

Maybe the pills would kill her over time; that was a pleasant thought to Wilhelmina. Maybe one day she could get her hands on the whole bottle and swallow them all before anyone could stop her. She would drift off into a pleasant slumber, away from the clock, and the carpet, and the motel room. They said in church that people who took their own lives were damned, but she didn't think she would be. She wasn't sure she hadn't already gone to hell.

There were other girls residing at the motel. She could hear them through the paper-thin walls sometimes, in those moments between Johns. But they certainly weren't allowed to meet. Those girls were forced to do the same things that she was forced to do. Wilhelmina often wondered who they were.

Where they came from. If they had loved ones who missed them, as she was sure her family missed her. She wondered how much more of this she could withstand before she lost her mind completely.

Now, she stopped dead in her tracks, on her way again to the nightstand drawer, as she heard the familiar sound of the opening door. She glanced around the room for something mundane to focus her attention on—cobwebs in a corner, a dust bunny on the carpet, semen stains on the headboard, anything but their faces. Anything to draw her attention from what was about to happen. The voices of men, one familiar, one not, talking as they entered her would-be prison cell. It was that time again. She'd spend the better part of the next 60 minutes forced to provide favors to a man she would never know, and likely never see again, while listening only to the sound of her life passing by, as narrated by the constant cadence of the ever-present clock.

*Tick tock ...*

# CHAPTER 6
# DRISKILL'S HARDWARE, TENNYSON COUNTY
PRESENT DAY

Tug Driskill was a lanky man with a potbelly sponsored by a nearly 12-pack-a-day habit of off-brand canned beer. The suits that he wore to work in his hardware store, which was located about a mile away from the Tennyson County landmark, Frog Rock, were throwbacks from the 1970s, but he prided himself on the fact that he could still squeeze into them. He smoked cigarettes one after another, leaving him smelling of burnt tobacco and tar, his fingers stained the color of dark urine from nicotine. He had a half halo of formerly red hair around his head, a thick mustache, reminiscent of an early 1980s porn actor, hiding his upper lip.

He had just been told that an old friend was here to see him, and he sat behind his gray metal desk waiting for his visitor. He lit his third smoke in 15 minutes, sat back in the swivel chair, and painted on the smile of a used car salesman. Looking around the room, whose walls were covered with faded framed awards from various business organizations, he thought, this is the life. This is certainly the life.

A knock on the door announced Jeremiah Waddell's arrival. The two men shook hands, left hands, as shaking with his right hand was an impossibility for Jeremiah, and sat across the desk from each other. They'd been friends since high school, neither man ever moving away from Tennyson County, but Tug's schedule at the store kept him from having much of a social life, not that he was often invited to attend many events anyway.

Once upon a time, Tug was a star football player in Tennyson County. His image regularly adorned the Sports section of the newspaper. He held multiple countywide records for his athletic achievements. Those days were gone; there were still some South Georgia natives who treated him like the hero he still felt he was. But they were growing fewer each year.

"Jeremiah Waddell, as I live and breathe. How long has it been, eight years? What the devil brings you my way this lovely afternoon?"

"Good to see ya, Tug. I'd like to say I'm just here to shoot the shit with ya, but that's only part of it," Jeremiah replied while trying not to inhale the tobacco smoke that was forming a cloud around the ceiling.

"Well, how's the family, Jeremiah? Cash doing good? That boy was quite the lady's man back in his teen years. He still chasing skirts and getting in trouble?

"Cash is Cash, Tug. I reckon that's neither good nor bad; it just is," Jeremiah Waddell answered with a nervous snicker.

"And little Annie? How's she doing these days without her Mama around?"

"Annie's fine, Tug. She don't do a whole lotta talkin', but we reckon she ain't got a lot to say."

"Good, good," said the hardware store owner. "Say, isn't that something, that murder up at the hotel? I don't think I can remember anything like that happening here in all my days."

"It's the damnedest thing if you ask me. That woman had a pocket rocket; did you hear that one?"

With a rolling belly laugh, Tug replied, "Hung like an African, she was. That's what everybody's saying, anyway."

"What is this world coming to?" Jeremiah responded with an anxious laugh of his own. "I don't reckon a tranny had any business in South Georgia to begin with, do you?"

"You can be honest with me, Jeremiah," Tug filtered a laugh through a gravelly cough, "she was here to see you, wasn't she?" With that, Tug Driskill nearly hacked up a lung while laughing at his old friend's expense.

Returning the laugh, but with far less commitment, Jeremiah replied, "That's funny, buddy, but I have a serious question for ya."

"Well, if this is a proposal, I'm afraid that I am already married, Jeremiah—"

"I need some work, Tug. I've spent the better part of the day asking anybody in the county with a payroll department to help me out, but they either don't have nothin' going, or they's afraid of Ruth Blakely, or both."

"Ha. Ol' Ruthless. That bitch ain't dead yet? She still

chasing pussy, or has she found herself a real man by now? What was it we used to say to crawl up under her skin?"

"Twofer," Jeremiah responded, though barely audible.

"What was that? I couldn't hear ya."

"TWOFER," Jeremiah repeated in a near yell, cringing at the word that sealed his doom for 50 years.

"That's right, twofer. Funniest damn thing I ever heard."

"Yeah, it's a stitch," Jeremiah said.

"I'll tell you what old friend, I just might have something parttime here in the store. If things work out, maybe we can expand your hours."

"No shit, Tug? But, what about Ruth?"

"That darkie dyke has nothing on me, Jeremiah. I am not the least bit afraid of her. If it's really a job you are after, whatcha say we get you started tomorrow morning?"

"That's mighty fine of ya, Tug. Tell me what time to be here, and I'll be here 10 minutes early."

The two men stood and shook hands. Jeremiah Wadell had saved this favor for a time when he had no choice; he knew he'd only get to use it just the once. But a job—a real one—had eluded him for a long time, and things weren't getting less complicated anytime soon. He reckoned it had been time to cash this one in. Maybe, he thought, it would even be the first stretch on his road to a legitimate life.

In the distance, the faint whistle of the G.R.I.T...

*Wooooooot*

# CHAPTER 7
# MAIN STREET, NOEWARE, GA

Nadine Bassette watched as Allison Edwards disappeared from view. From somewhere deep inside her blouse, her cell phone rang, and the madam fetched it from its cradle in her bra strap. "This is Nadine—"

The voice on the other end of the phone was frantic. This was the third such call from this same person in the past four days. Nadine was growing weary of having the same conversation over and over. She listened politely for a few moments before interrupting.

"Deidre, Sugar, we have been over this until I am sick of talking about it. I told you that if I run into Allison, I won't say a word. The truth is, I have yet to meet your daughter, so you have nothing to worry about so far. I have things to do today, so I can't spend all afternoon on the phone with you trying to ease your mind. You know you can trust me, Hun. Your secret's safe."

She rolled her eyes as the woman continued for a few minutes more, then replied, "Uh huh. Yeah. Well, keep your pretty hair pretty, Sugar—," because she had no idea what else to say.

Down the road, Billy Washington caught up with Allison Edwards. Nearly out of breath, Billy said, "G.H., you went all Krystle Carrington on that boy. I was waiting for you to fling him in the mud."

Stopping in mid-step and turning to Billy, Allison responded, "Is that supposed to make sense?"

"You know, Dynasty. Oh Lawd, never mind, G.H., you really were a PBS child growing up, weren't you?"

Giggling at the slight, Allison responded, "It was hard to beat Sesame Street and Electric Company, Billy."

Following a good laugh, which both Billy and Allison desperately needed, Allison nodded up the street—

"Billy, who is that woman? You know, the one with the pink hair and Cadillac?

"Ohhhhhh, that, G.H., is Miss Nadine Bassette. That woman done rose to the top by getting down—a lot."

"You mean—"

"Uh-huh, it's just like that Bobbie and Rubie on General Hospital years ago."

Allison, staring at the older woman but shaking her head at Billy, replied, "I don't know what that even means, but I can guess."

"Uh huh," Billy said, "they say that years ago, some men from the county government approached Miss Nadine and asked her to open her establishment."

"No. Seriously?"

"That's what they say. They figured that all these transient farm workers had a better chance of staying in town for a while if they had some entertainment."

"You mean—"

"That's right, G.H., Orlando, Florida has Disney World, Tennyson County, Georgia has Nadine's Boarding House."

Nadine Bassette ended her call with Deidre Edwards and immediately dialed a number listed in her contacts. The call was answered on the first ring.

"Hey, Sugar, it's Nadine. Our old friend will be visiting tomorrow afternoon, and you know that you are the only one that he'll see." Listening to the reply from the other end of the phone, Nadine responded, "Great, I'll get back to you with the details."

Billy and Allison continued their conversation as they walked past the flower shop owned by the Wei family. Carol Wei, the family matriarch who ran the shop, appeared to have just been approached by one of the many F.B.I. agents in town investigating Jessica Walters' murder. After a few brief words, the agent walked away, and Billy and Allison approached.

"Well," Allison said to Carol, "I see the F.B.I. is leaving no one out of its investigation. No stone unturned, as they say."

"I'm sorry?" Carol replied, looking confused and a bit distracted.

"We saw the F.B.I. agent speaking with you," Allison responded.

"I'm quite sure that you're mistaken," Carol said. "It's sure nice to see you on the mend, Billy," she added before she turned and walked back inside her shop, leaving Billy Washington and Allison Edwards looking at each other perplexed.

# CHAPTER 8
# WASHINGTON RESIDENCE, TENNYSON COUNTY

Cora Washington was screwing the cap onto a canning jar full of stewed tomatoes, in deep thought about the current happenings around town, when her kitchen door opened, startling her back to reality. A stray speck of metal caused a small cut to her hand, "Well, I'll be a suck-egg mule," she said, grabbing a dish towel to wrap around the bleed. Billy Washington and Ruth Blakely entered the kitchen, which was filled with the acidic aroma of fresh stewed vegetables and steam from boiling water pots.

"I never understood that saying," Ruth Blakey said, looking in her sister's direction before using her walker to assist her to a chair at the kitchen table. With a pained expression on her face, the mayor lowered herself to a seated position and shook her head at what appeared to be 50 canning jars filled to the rim. "You'll not finish all of these before you die of old age, Cora."

"By the time I am ready to go, Ruthie, you'll be worm

food, so I guess you won't be needing to worry about it," Cora responded to her older sister while kissing the woman on the top of her head.

Billy chuckled at the banter between his auntie and his mother, while noticing that Cora was dressed more formally than usual under her apron. "Mama, you look like that Miss Ellie from Dallas headed to the Oil Baron's Ball, why are you so dressed up?"

"Shut up, boy. Miss Ellie ain't never waited for double coupon day at the Piggly Wiggly to go grocery shopping like I'll be doing after I stop by Mama's house."

"Oh, you're going by the Honey Hole this afternoon?" Billy replied.

"No, WE are going to Mama Jo's house, me and you. Although, I think it would be nice if the three of us went. There is no telling how much longer Mama will be with us. I'd venture to say that she doesn't have a lot of time left. You two are about 20 minutes later getting here than you said you'd be, one hopes she held on this long."

"Oh, PLEASE," Ruth responded, "that damn woman has been on hospice since Diana Ross was a Supreme. She is going nowhere soon. You can blame me for our tardiness. I seem to have misplaced my watch."

"I have been telling you for ages that you had better get that clasp fixed, or you were gonna lose that thing. Dagnabbit, Ruthie, that watch is about the nicest thing you own. I hope you find it," Cora sighed.

"Mama, is that quilt you made me still in the hall linen closet? It won't be long before the weather changes, and I'd like to put it on my bed," Billy asked, reminding the women that he was still in the room.

"No, baby, it's in the closet in the spare room. I'll go—"

"I've got it, mama; you put a bandage on that cut before you bleed out."

Billy headed toward the hallway to retrieve the quilt. Ruth waited until she was sure that he was out of earshot before addressing her sister, "That man has been abused enough in the past few days, don't you think, Cora? Do not subject him to that woman, too."

"I'll remind you that that woman is his granny, and she hasn't seen him in a month of Sundays."

"His granny can barely stand the sight of him, Cora, and you know that I am not going over there, either."

"You are going to regret that decision when it's too late, Ruth Blakely. It's not like I am asking you to take a gift basket to Uncle J.B. at the pork plant."

"HOG FARM! And you know better than to mention that man's name to me."

"Alright, Ruth, suit yourself. I'll go see Mama alone. You'll need Billy to drive you back into town anyway."

"Now, Cora, let's get real for a minute. I know you didn't insist that I visit so that I could help you can tomatoes. A domestic goddess I am not. And if it was a ruse to get me to go see that woman, you just gave in awfully fast. What's really going on?"

"I could ask you the very same question, Ruth. Carl told me how upset you got about the stories he has been running in the paper. It ain't like you to get personally involved in the newspaper business."

"Go on—"

I've also known for a while that you put up the 'grant' money that brought Allison Edwards to Noeware, too. That didn't make a lick of sense to me either."

"Mmm hmm—"

"Well, when I put those two things together, it got me thinking about other things. Like, I knew when we were kids that it wasn't normal for a poor colored girl from South Georgia to go to Atlanta and live with rich folks. AND it doesn't take a genius to see that Jessica Walters was at least part black. Nor that she happened to have the Blakely chin. Which you also got a heaping helping of. I may not have a fancy law degree like you, but our Mama never raised a fool. So, is there anything that YOU want to talk about?"

"No," Ruth replied with just a touch of venom in her voice; Cora was her sister, so she wouldn't use all she was capable of—but she wouldn't keep it all back, either.

Sighing loudly, exasperated and disappointed, Cora said, "Billy, I don't think your auntie is feeling very well. Why don't you take her on home? I think I've had enough of her company for one day."

Billy's eyes were as wide as dinner plates as he stood in the kitchen doorway, "I'll meet you outside, Auntie." With that, he left the house, that suddenly felt frigid, despite the smoldering temperature from the running stove.

"Cora, you need not focus your anger on me when you should be focusing your concern in the direction of your son. Did it ever occur to you that it seldom gets cold enough in Tennyson County for one to need a quilt of that weight on his bed? Or that after years of living on his own, he suddenly needs his mother to supply a blanket?"

"What are you getting at, Ruth?"

"Comfort, Cora, the man needs comfort. You and Carl aren't providing it, as he is too busy reporting on this Noeware Man nonsense, and you are too busy taking care of Cruella de Vil. You two have left William to cling on to whatever he can. You sit here, all self-righteous, and interrogate me like a suspect in a crime—like a common criminal. You think you have everything figured out, and you may not be far off, but what you want to know is MY business, no one else's."

"Now wait—"

"No, you listen to me, little sister. I am about a half second away from asking you for a comfort quilt of my own. And you may have noticed that my job has gotten an awful lot harder in the last few days. Now is not the time. When I am ready to talk, you'll be one of the first to know. But I'll be damned if I will tolerate you being angry at me when what I need right now is your support."

Cora Washington, tears forming in her eyes, placed both of her hands over both of Ruth's and squeezed with the firm grip of unconditional love. Despite the lack of affirmation, her suspicions had been confirmed. No further words were needed—none were spoken.

# CHAPTER 9
# CRABAPPLE LANE, TENNYSON COUNTY

Crabapple Lane was on the outskirts of Tennyson County. Over the years, it had taken on the nickname, though most would call it a slur, of the Honey Hole. Historically, the neighborhood had been the home of most of Tennyson County's black population. The streets, paved with Georgia red clay, were lined with boarded-up mill houses, otherwise known as *shotgun shacks* for the way one room led to another straight down a central hall. The design allowed a breeze to flow from the front of the house to the back, in the days before air conditioning. Of course, nobody these days would leave their doors unlocked all day in that part of town; not that many of the houses were still occupied. Some of the houses had absentee owners, mostly grandchildren and great-grandchildren living in other parts of the state who were participating in various stages of neglect and abandonment, having found themselves unable to sell. Nobody in their right mind was going to spend money on those properties for another 20 years when they'd be purchased together and razed for a new rendering plant. At the moment, the area was nearly abandoned completely, except for a petty criminal or two running unsavory operations and for number 6, the home of Jolene "Mama Jo" Blakely.

The outside of the basic cream-colored house, sided with wooden slats that were chipped and weathered and slowly turning to the same driftwood grey, was standard for the neighborhood. There was a small front porch with no railing other than some boxwood hedges that had been allowed to overgrow and cover half the windows and a tiny postage stamp-sized front lawn that was more plain dirt than grass or even weeds.

Inside, the noise was nearly unbearable. The television volume was blaring loudly, The Price is Right currently on. A radio, volume set on 10, played church hymns continuously, in competition with the T.V. Mama Jo, an oxygen mask covering both her nose and mouth, lay in a hospital bed in the living room, seemingly oblivious to the sounds around her, while nurse Rhonda Conner attended to her.

"Mrs. Blakely, you are still able to get out of this bed. Your toilet seat is right here beside you. Why do you still soil your diaper?" the nurse asked.

"I ain't doin' your job for you, girl. Jesus washed feet. Are you sayin' you're too good to clean me up?" the old woman replied sharply.

"I'm not saying that at all, Mrs. Blakely. I just thought that since you are capable, you would want—"

"Ain't nobody payin' you to think, girl, we're payin' you to work. Now, quit all that talkin' and get to it."

Nurse Conner rolled the octogenarian over onto her right side so that she could remove the adult diaper currently being worn by the most ill-tempered patient that she had ever worked with, and she'd worked with some real donkeys over the years. She was too polite to call them anything else, even in her own mind, though Mrs. Blakely surely tempted her. Using baby wipes, she cleaned urine from the old woman and applied a lotion to prevent a rash. Without any assistance from Mama Jo, she applied a new undergarment and cleaned up the area around the bed.

"Therefore, since Christ suffered in his body, arm yourselves also with the same attitude, because whoever suffers in body is done with sin, 1 Peter 4:1," Mama Jo added. "For our light and momentary troubles are achieving for us an eternal glory that far outweighs them all, 2 Corinthians 4:17."

Rhonda Conner sighed.

The front door opened with a bang, as the Georgia humidity caused it to swell in its frame. Cora Washington entered the house carrying a bouquet of carnations, shook her head, and smiled apologetically at Rhonda Conner. "How's the patient today?"

"I'm your Mama; I ain't your patient. Why don't you open some of these curtains so as I can see outside? Those flowers better not have come from them Japs."

"Mama," Cora replied, "you wouldn't be able to see anything out those windows anyway; the shrubs are too tall. Why don't you let me get Billy to come over and trim them for you? And the Wei family is Chinese, not Japanese, and that term is racist."

"I don't need that fairy to do anything for me. As sick as I am, I'd probably get some nasty person's disease just from being around him. And I don't care where them slant eyes are from, they ain't Americans is all I know. Racist? Don't talk to me about racist."

"Mama, that's rude and uncalled for. You are going to keep that up and run away any help you get from anybody."

"Go on then, G.E.T.," Mama Jo barked. "Just leave me here to rot in my own piss. I don't need any of y'all anyway."

Cora shook her head while she tried to lower the volume on the bedside radio.

"Don't touch that radio. I need my music since ain't none of y'all tried to take me to church in ages."

"She turns the volume up on the T.V. and radio so that she can't hear the hiss of the oxygen tank. I've told her that the washer needs to be replaced," Rhonda said loudly into Cora's ear.

"Mama, it's not safe for you to be in here with a leaky oxygen tank. We'll have someone come and look at it for you."

"I ain't lettin' nobody in this house, girl. There ain't nothin' wrong with that tank, and I want all y'all to quit your fussin'; it just gets me riled up. You'd invite some thievin' trash into my home? Well, ain't that just somethin'?"

"Well," Cora responded while shaking her head, "someone may need to be here for a while. I just don't think it's safe for you to be here alone, not with a killer prowling around."

"I can take care of my damn self, girl," Mama Jo replied around a wicked cough.

Leaving the living room and heading towards the kitchen, Cora said a little prayer for patience, loud enough for only

God to hear. She opened the refrigerator and placed the lunch that she had packed for her mother inside.

"Mama," Cora yelled as loud as she could, to be heard over the T.V. and radio, "You are taking too many of your pain pills. You should have about twice as many as I see in this bottle."

Mama Jo ignored Cora completely, keeping her focus on the wheel spinning on the T.V. gameshow, pausing momentarily to remove her oxygen mask to cough violently.

In the kitchen, Cora tried to open the back door. Pressing her entire body against it, she thrust it open on the third attempt. Outside, on the stoop next to the door, was an old wooden cane chair; a vintage ashtray stood beside it, its bowl overflowing with cigarette butts. Cora shook her head at the discovery. Turning around to head back inside, she bumped into Rhonda Conner in the doorway.

"I'm not understanding your mama these days," the nurse said to Cora. "She won't get out of bed to relieve herself, but she'll come out here to smoke. Before I washed her bed linens yesterday, they were stained with feces, though she never let me know that she had had an accident."

"I swanny," Cora responded, shaking her head, "sometimes I have doubts that her accidents are actually accidents."

Both women giggled.

"I can't figure out when she comes out here to smoke," Cora replied. "It seems like between my visits a few times a day and you coming over to check on her, one of us would see her."

"It's a mystery for sure," Rhonda said with a look of worry on her face.

"Rhonda, I don't mean to pry, but are you okay? Only, you look a little more stressed than usual. If Mama is getting to be too much—"

"Oh no, it's not your Mama. Well, I mean, she is a bit extra, but I have a different situation going on at home that is weighing on me."

"I'm sorry to hear that. Anything that I can help you with?"

"Oh no, I don't want to worry you with my problems. My roommate's problem, really; she's going through some things. She paused, her brows creasing deeper. With a shrug, she cleared her face and said, with a notable lack of confidence, "Well, anyway, I think she'll be okay …"

"I understand," Cora said while rubbing the shoulder of the younger nurse. "I'm here if you need to talk. It'd be nice if someone took me up on my offer to listen one of these days."

"I sure appreciate that, Cora. I promise to take you up on that offer if things get worse."

They stood for a moment longer, each lost in their respective thoughts, before turning and going back into the house to face the wrath of Mama Jo. Neither woman was aware of a set of ears listening to every word spoken between them, just on the other side of the overgrown back hedge.

The G.R.I.T. passed as the women walked back inside.

*Wooooooot*

## CHAPTER 10
## THE G.R.I.T. DEPOT, NOEWARE, GA

Under the high ceiling of the depot's lobby, Allison bent at the knees to kneel and scratch the head of Dewie, the ever-present orange tabby cat who seemed—by her own preference—to belong to the town at large. Dewie's loud purr and beatific look thanked her for the adoration, though there was no meow—there never was. Allison returned to a standing position and made her way toward an older gentleman in pin-striped overalls, painting on a canvas propped against a well-used easel. In any other town, this scene would appear noteworthy; in Noeware, Georgia, it just meant that R.W. was hard at work.

"Good afternoon, R.W., it's good to see you again," Allison said.

"Well, afternoon, young Allison. It's a mighty fine thing to receive a visit from you, as well."

Allison giggled as she took a seat in one of the depot lobby's worn but still polished benches, "I don't know about young; these four-decade-old bones are creaking pretty loudly today."

"Get back with me in about 20 years, young lady; we'll talk about creaking bones," R.W. replied while holding a spot on his lower back. "I sure was sorry to hear about that poor Jessica. How are you holdin' up?"

"About as well as you can imagine," Allison said, a defeated look on her face, "I'm still in shock and, if I'm honest, completely bewildered."

"Ahhhh," R.W. offered, already aware of Allison's state of mind, "I reckon you would be, what with her havin' a husband and all."

"Ha," Allison said halfheartedly, "as usual, word travels fast around here."

"That it does, that it does. How long do you reckon you'll be in town?"

"Well, I suppose that's up to the authorities. They are still ruling out the spouse, and I guess I am considered one of them," Allison said, still in disbelief.

The two sat in relative silence for a few moments, while R.W. focused intently on his current painting, canvas facing himself as usual, no one else privy to his work. With a flourish, he made a final stroke with his paint brush, and sighed at the finished product.

"I don't suppose you'll allow me a glance at your latest work of art?"

"In due time, Allison Edwards, all in due time. Now, get it off your chest, that pressure that's building. I reckon I can feel it from over here."

"You know, R.W., you may just be the most observant

man that I have ever met. The truth is, I can't get past the stunning coincidence that Jess arrives in town and is almost immediately killed. It couldn't have been random, but there is absolutely no explanation for it." Tears forming in her eyes, a lump in her throat, Allison tried to continue, "Obviously, Jess was keeping something from me, something huge, and I can't tell if I am more mad at her about that or about her leaving me here alone." She stopped, grief sticking in her throat. R.W. remained gently silent while she gathered herself. "And maybe if I'd found out about her HUSBAND while she was alive, I'd have been mad enough to think about wanting her dead. But only in theory, not in practice! Whatever she was hiding, she didn't deserve to die, not like that, and not in a place where she had no ties. Please don't take offense at this, but a place like Noeware?? Why was she here at all? The entire situation is just unfathomable—senseless."

"Well, I reckon the first thing that you need to understand, Allison Edwards, is that there are no such things as coincidences. Nothing happens by chance. What is supposed to be will invariably be. Ever considered that your venture to Noeware wasn't about Jessica, whether she had ties here or not? Perhaps, maybe she was about to get in the way of YOUR purpose, your destiny if you will."

Stunned, Allison looked at the man in disbelief. "Are you saying that you think that *I* have ties to Noeware, Georgia? That's ridiculous. I have never been here before. I came here after winning a journalism contest." She shook her head. That ridiculous article about Noeware. It had only been a few days ago, but it felt like a different Allison who'd been offered the chance to write it.

"Well, maybe you're right. What do I know, anyhow? After all, I am just an old man with a paintbrush and back trouble. It's quite possible that I ain't got a lick of sense. I certainly weren't a scholar back in my school days. In fact, I had a little trouble completing tasks back then and couldn't seem to hang around in one place long enough. But I digress—"

"R.W., speaking of not being able to hang around—"

"Yes ma'am, you have somewhere that you need to be."

Standing up from her seat while watching Dewie circle the old man's leg, Allison finished, "You know, somehow, I think that if I sat here for years talking to you, I still wouldn't be any closer to figuring out how you stay one step ahead of everything."

"Experience leads to knowledge, Allison Edwards, and with age comes experience. Including hard experience."

R.W. watched as the front door of the depot swung shut with Allison's exit. He allowed himself one more sigh, as he looked at his finished painting. The scene filled him with concern. Wires, monitors, doctors, nurses, and a patient in a bed. This wasn't good, it certainly wasn't good at all.

## CHAPTER 11
## MIDDLE OF NOEWARE DINER, NOEWARE, GA

Claire Montgomery took the cup of coffee from the hand of Ned Wilson after receiving the change from a five-dollar bill. "Ned, if this coffee isn't decaf, I swear I will be paying you a visit at two in the morning when I am unable to sleep."

"Slinging food and coffee has been my career for a lifetime, Claire. I reckon I can tell the difference between regular and unleaded," he replied with a laugh.

With a grin for her niece's ex-husband, of whom she was very fond, Claire turned from the counter and almost walked directly into Police Chief Ernie Thomas. "Well, Ernie, you were almost wearing this cup of coffee."

"I sure am glad to run into you, Claire, no pun intended. You have a quick minute?"

"A very quick one. I have a lot to do, as I am sure you can imagine."

"Ned, mind bringing a cup of regular in a paper cup over to the booth when you get a sec?"

Ned nodded by way of reply, and Chief Thomas and Claire Montgomery took a seat in a nearby booth.

"Claire, I'll just get right to it, there is a thing or two that I need to clear up in my head, with regards to our chat at the hotel the other night."

"Ernie, I feel like I have been over this until I am blue in the face. What is left, for God's sake?"

"Just before Gail joined us in the office the other night, you asked where she had been. The officer upstairs said that she had been unconscious in the closet."

"I am fully aware of what I said, Ernie. Why don't you get to the point?"

"Well, your reply to that news was, and I quote, 'In the closet, that's par for the course in this town'."

"Your point is?"

"I'll get back to that in a second. Suppose you tell me again why Daisy Wei had been on the scene at the hotel and basically in the middle of everything when she had called in sick that evening."

"Ernie, there is no mystery there, we called Daisy in to work because we needed all available personnel in the emergency situation."

"Ahh, I see. That makes a lot of sense to me. Except, you had Gail on shift, yet Daisy was doing the heavy lifting, making phone calls to rehouse your guests."

"Yes, because we couldn't find Gail and needed to make the re-arrangements."

"So," Ernie Thomas asked with a quizzical look, "instead

of looking for your niece, who was already on shift and in a position of authority, you called in Daisy Wei, who is often confused about which shoe goes on which foot?"

As a thin layer of sweat formed on Claire Montgomery's forehead, she replied, "You don't go into battle with the army you wished you had, Ernie. You fight with the troops who are available."

"Fight. That's an interesting word choice, Claire. Let's get back to the 'par for the course' comment, shall we?"

"Ernie, this is growing very tiresome—"

"I just think it's interesting that you suggest that folks around here might be 'in the closet' when the very night before the murder, an assault took place in an alley known for gay cruising, an assault carried out by the same suspect that we like for Jessica Walter's murder."

"The murderer is a nazi skinhead, Ernie. Is it that shocking?"

"It probably wouldn't be if your niece Meg's husband wasn't just arrested last night in that very same alley for public indecency, suggesting that the good doctor might, indeed, 'be in the closet'."

"Are you suggesting that I or anyone in my family had anything to do with any of the crimes committed in this town in the last few days, Ernie Thomas? May I remind you, it was Billy Washington, and not Don Givens, who was assaulted? Moreover, I'd like to know if you plan to interrogate me in a diner in the future, so that I may make sure to plan ahead."

"I can't really suggest anything, Claire. This case is in the hands of the F.B.I., and we're just having a friendly conversation. However, I'd probably put some thought into some of the things we've discussed if I were you."

Meanwhile, outside the diner ...

Nadine Bassette was headed towards the diner door, when she was approached by Allison Edwards. They reached for the door at the same time, both stopping in mid-grasp.

"I'm sorry, after you, Hun," Nadine said to the younger woman.

"Oh no, please—"

"Well, if you insist."

Before Nadine could enter the diner, Allison added, "Actually, I am really glad that I ran into you. I wanted to thank you for your kindness earlier today. It meant a lot to me."

"Oh, think nothing of it, Sugar, us women have to stick together."

"All the same, I appreciate it. You know, people told me some things about you when I first got here, and I can't say I approve of what you do. From a feminist standpoint, that is. I can't say I think it could be good for women, even women who don't have a lot of options, to do what ... the women in your house do. And I admit to being wary about you at first. But you've really changed those expectations, and I genuinely appreciate you being there."

Smiling, Nadine responded, "Oh, Sugar, I've sought a lot in life—money, love, happiness, but I've never sought approval. Not from anyone, let alone a stranger from Atlanta."

"Oh, I didn't mean—"

"I think I know exactly what you meant, Hun. You might want to spend a little time dusting your own shelves before you give mine the white glove treatment. You may also want to consider how many people in the world can carry on just fine without ever knowing your opinion of them."

With that, the madam entered the diner and left Allison Edwards standing on the sidewalk, stewing in her own embarrassment.

"Allison?" Dr. Meg Givens said as she approached, "Are you okay?"

"Meg, I'm sorry, I guess I am just a little exhausted from the happenings over the past few days."

At the same moment, Dr. Jerri Hansard approached the two women on the sidewalk and asked, "Are you two ladies going inside, or are you the impromptu doorpersons?"

"Good evening, Dr. Hansard—we meet again," Meg said.

"Hi Meg. Oh, I'm Jerri Hansard," the woman said, holding out her hand in introduction to Allison.

"Hansard? My God, your son is—"

"Dr. Hansard, this is Allison Edwards," Meg said, feeling the embarrassment of all three women.

"Shit," Jerri responded, "I can't seem to catch a break today. Yes, I am the mother of the infamous Noeware Man. I hope you'll not hold that against me."

"No," Allison replied, "I'm very tired, and I know you had nothing to do with this terrible situation. Look, ladies," Allison continued, changing the subject, "do you think Hank would mind taking me to get a rental car? It looks like I'll be here for a while."

"Hank?" Jerri Hansard responded.

"Long story," Meg Givens replied.

"I know this may sound crazy; we've known each other for about two and a half seconds now, but I could certainly use a few hours away from town. I'd be happy to go get a rental car for you. That seems like the very least that I could do, considering—" Jerri said.

"Hours?" Allison replied in surprise.

"I'm afraid so," Meg said, "the nearest rental car place that is likely to actually have an available car is at least several hours away. I don't know how the F.B.I. would feel about you taking a day trip, and you," now turning to Jerri Hansard, "will need someone to go with you."

"It can't be you, Meg, and you know exactly why that is out of the question," Jerri responded matter-of-factly. She had been through enough over the past few days, she didn't need a car-ride with a patient's wife to be seen as a possible breach of confidentiality. Especially given the attention that particular patient had received since the day before.

"Well, you'll have to push me out of the passenger's seat of your car. I need a little time away from here, too." Turning to Allison, she continued, "Now, you promise me that you'll get a health screen tomorrow morning. I'll call and let someone know you're coming. I realize that you've been under a lot of stress, but Gail says that you've fainted twice in just a few days' time. That's not normal."

"I'm okay," Allison said, thinking that nothing that had happened since she first entered this town had been normal.

"No arguments," Meg interrupted.

"Okay," Allison agreed, resigning from the need to see a doctor. "But, if it's going to take all day tomorrow, you really can't be the one to go to get a car. Your dad's campaign announcement is tomorrow evening."

"We can leave early, and we'll be back in plenty of time for the announcement, right, Jerri?" Meg assured Allison.

Sighing heavily, Jerri Hansard agreed, realizing that this wasn't a battle that she was going to win. Anyway, if they left early enough, maybe nobody would notice them leaving town together.

Just then, the rattle of metal walker legs caused Meg to turn her attention toward the woman passing by. "Ahhh, Mayor Blakely, I see you have been left without plans for Founders' Day Weekend, too. What about the festivities being canceled? It's a real shame, don't you think?"

Stopping abruptly on the sidewalk beside the three women, Ruth replied, "Perhaps you should focus on kennel training your husband so that he doesn't stray into dark alleys at night, and leave the city's business to me, Dr. Givens. Nodding towards Allison, Ruth added, "I'll see you shortly, Ms. Edwards."

Continuing down the street, Mayor Ruth Blakely stopped for a brief word with Miss Willa, who was sitting on a bench, her ever-present suitcase next to her on its roller, a bible in her lap. "Good evening, Willa. Think we'll see any more rain? Say, you haven't found a watch on your travels, have you? I seem to have misplaced mine."

"Watch? I can't say that I have. I'll be looking for it, though. Oh Ruthie, have you seen my little girl?" the woman replied, signs of hope in her eyes, which was the only thing to add light to a face sagging from years of pain and physical hardship. She held up an old photograph of Tina Hansard.

Inside the diner, Nadine Bassette took her to-go bag from Ned Wilson and said, "I sure appreciate it, Sugar. Y'all be careful out here, there's a killer on the loose." Glancing around, she raised her voice to be clearly heard, "Although, I don't think the authorities need to look much further than the Waddell house, do y'all?"

Sitting in a corner booth, Cash Waddell sat with a face turning the color of a pickled beet, fire in his eyes. Nadine winked at him on the way out the door. "Evening, Cash." Nadine smiled and nodded at the man who held the door for her, "My appreciation, Bruce."

## CHAPTER 12
## MAYOR'S OFFICE, NOEWARE, GA

Ruth Blakely sat in the chair behind her desk, her walker nearby, as Allison Edwards and Ernie Thomas entered the office. They each took seats across from the mayor, averting their eyes from each other, the friction between them palpable.

"Good evening, Allison, Ernie," Ruth greeted, "we are waiting on one more."

No sooner had the mayor finished her sentence, than Dennis Hernandez entered the office and took a standing position behind Allison and Ernie.

"Oh, you've got to be kidding," Allison said.

"What I have to say concerns the three of you, Allison," Ruth replied. "I asked Chief Thomas to invite Mr. Hernandez."

"Why are we here, Ruth?" Ernie Thomas asked. "Don't you think any conversations among the two of them should have the F.B.I. in attendance, given they've elected to manage the investigation?"

"Thank you for your input, Chief Thomas. I've scheduled an interview with the F.B.I. tomorrow. However, it's time I came clean about a few things that affect Mr. Hernandez and Ms. Edwards. I felt it important to explain the situation to all of you before informing the officials."

"We're listening," Allison Edwards said, shifting in her chair.

Taking a deep breath, Ruth began. "When I was just 16 years old, I found myself in a family way. At that time, this may not have been a big deal in a big city like Atlanta or Indianapolis," she nodded first towards Allison, then Dennis, "where at least a family could expect some anonymity if they chose it. But in Noeware, as small as it was and still is, and in the Bible Belt, it was not only unacceptable, it was a permanent stigma."

Allison Edwards attempted to hide her astonishment. Ruth Blakely, a mother? Ruthless Ruth? The woman whose body temperature must rival the coldness of a reptile? This couldn't be real. Ernie, on the other hand, made no such attempt. He'd known Ruth Blakely for 50 years and had never heard her acknowledge a weakness of any kind. Dennis Hernandez was merely mystified, unsure how a teenage pregnancy decades ago in Georgia could be relevant to him.

Ruth continued, "Arrangements were made for my child to be adopted by a lovely couple in Atlanta. They were fine people, lawyers, law professors."

Allison's eyes began to widen as the point of the mayor's confession was starting to sink in.

"They were an interracial couple, weren't they, Ruth?" Allison asked, voice low.

"I can't believe what I am hearing," Dennis Hernandez interjected, arriving at the same conclusion.

"That's right, they were," Ruth continued, tears reaching the surface of her lower eyelids. "Their last name was Walters, and they raised a little boy who never should have been born that way."

Ernie Thomas interrupted, "Are you telling me—"

"I am not finished, Ernie; there will be plenty of time for your questions when I am done," Ruth admonished.

"So, you are telling me that you are ..." began Dennis again, more loudly this time.

"IF you are all quite through, I happen not to be," Ruth said yet louder, trying to maintain her composure. "The Walters and I remained quite close over the years. They kept me abreast of most of the details of Jessica's life. It certainly sounded as if they had done a stellar job at raising their daughter. Their daughter whom I had never met."

"Oh my God," Allison exclaimed, a new realization hitting her. "That newspaper grant. Was that just your way of attempting to lure Jessica here through me? Like a fish to a hook?"

"I wouldn't express it in those exact words, but you certainly seem to get the point," Ruth said evenly, not admonishing her for the interruption this time.

Ernie Thomas wiped his hand over his face, realizing that this confession made the mayor a murder suspect. Before he could say anything, Allison Edwards continued, a new thought occurring to her.

"And I suppose my article about Anniston was just a ruse? To think I thought my writing actually caught someone's attention. All those ridiculous interviews I've been running around doing, were they for nothing?"

"Your story was quite good, Allison. Your writing ability was an added bonus."

"Jesus Christ!" she said, more coldly now. "You know, she would never in a million years come to this god-forsaken place if it weren't for you. You're the reason she's dead, whether you did it yourself or not," Allison added.

"Enough, girl," the mayor said in a firm voice, continuing slowly and enunciating each word. "I am laying the story out for all of you because it is the right thing to do, but I'll be damned if I will sit here and be lectured by my daughter's side piece."

Shooting out of her seat, Allison leaned over the mayor's desk to look her directly in the eyes, "How dare you. You've been lying to us and everyone around you. You set us all up for ... What reason, I can't even imagine? And you have the balls to sit there judging me? You are nothing but a selfish bitch, a disgusting little fish in a shit town thinking you have the right to pull all our strings. I wish I had never heard of you or of Noeware. If I hadn't, Jess would still be ..." At last, her ire melted back into grief. She sat back down, waiting for the next shoe to drop.

"What I don't understand," Dennis Hernandez said quietly in the silence that followed, "is how you knew that Jessica and I would come to Noeware."

"I had no idea, Mr. Hernandez, just like the Walters had no idea that you existed."

"What?" Dennis Hernandez said, trailing off and folding himself into a seated position on the office floor, unable to continue standing.

"Jessica's parents, of course, know all about Allison, and in fact, they care for her deeply. They were never told about you or about any marriage," Ruth responded.

"Jess told me that they were dead."

Allison looked at Dennis and seemed to find a source of some compassion for him, something she'd been struggling to do for the last few days. "They aren't dead, Dennis, but they do find it hard to travel these days. They're both elderly and live with full-time assistance. If they had known about you, I still doubt they could have made it to Indiana."

"Jess and I were just coming to town to explain everything to Allison. Jessica thought the timing was right since they'd be away from home—but I didn't think ..."

"Didn't think what, Dennis?" Allison said, her empathy for him evaporating with the reminder that he'd apparently known all about her while she had been kept in the dark. "Are you surprised to learn she was keeping things from you, too? And why on earth would you choose now—in Noeware of all places—to tell me that my life partner has been lying to me for years? Did you think I'd make less of a scene here?"

"Something like that," Dennis confessed.

"Well, if there is nothing else, this is a lot to swallow," Ernie Thomas said, reminding them all that he was in the room. He stood and headed towards the door.

"I appreciate your time, Ernie," Ruth Blakely said as the police chief left the office.

Now, standing himself, Dennis Hernandez made his way

towards the door. "Allison, I am so sorry about all of this. Maybe we can catch up with each other tomorrow and talk things over." He walked out, shaking his head in disbelief.

Allison, who was already standing, made her way toward the door but stopped abruptly, "I guess R.W. was right. There really are no coincidences."

"STOP!" Ruth shouted. "You and I aren't finished, Ms. Edwards. Close the door and have a seat, please."

Later, Allison would wonder what could be next. She sat alone on a bench in front of city hall, the same bench, in fact, that had been her refuge after her last shocking meeting with Ruth Blakely just a few days ago. The conversation about Jessica's parentage had been difficult, but the revelation that followed left her struggling to catch her breath. She wished that Meg was around, half worried that she'd faint again. Maybe Meg was right, and she should be worried about her health. And here she was, without the person who cared most for her. She was lost, stuck in a town where she was connected to nobody, and nobody cared for her. Well, she thought ruefully, strike that. Apparently, all kinds of people knew her here. She just didn't have the benefit of knowing anything about them. Noeware was her curse, and she'd be cursed to stay here for at least a little while. For the first time in a day, she thought of her home in Atlanta and longed to return, to just get away from here and back home, before remembering that it would be empty when she got there. Why had she ever come here, she wondered. And when she finally got to leave, where would she go?

*Woooooot*

# CHAPTER 13
# MIDDLE OF NOEWARE DINER, NOEWARE, GA

"Billy. Those trash bags are still sitting by the back door. They aren't going to take themselves out to the dumpster," Ned Wilson shouted over the loud music playing in the diner. After hours, Billy Washington often cranked the music up while he cleaned.

"I heard you the first eight times you reminded me, Ned. I told you that I'd get to them."

"See that you do, please. I about tripped over them twice."

Sweat forming on the palms of his hands, Billy made his way back to the bags. He took a deep breath before opening the door leading to the back alley where the industrial dumpster was located. His heart raced as he stepped into the dark night and toward the trash receptacle. Opening the door on the side of the dumpster, he lifted the heavy bags one at a time, tossing each one inside. He suddenly jumped as something brushed past his foot. Dewie, the town's orange tabby cat, was in pursuit of something.

"Lawd, Billy, get a grip on yourself," he said out loud, needing to hear a human voice, even if it was his own.

Closing the dumpster's door, he heard a crash from behind him. Could it have been Dewie, he thought? Whatever had fallen, it was much too large and heavy for Dewie to have budged it.

Ned Wilson stepped outside the diner's door, which had been left wide-open, and saw his co-worker and friend sitting on the stoop.

"Billy, what in the hell are you doing—" he started to ask, before realizing that Billy was sobbing uncontrollably.

Taking a seat next to Billy, Ned placed his arm around him. "Are you alright?"

"Someone was out here. I am sure that someone was out here."

Ned wasn't sure whether Billy had seen or heard anyone. Perhaps this reaction was a result of the man's trauma from the assault he experienced a few nights ago. To Ned, it really didn't matter. Billy was completely beside himself, and Ned was glad that he could take up his other side. He pulled Billy close, allowing him to rest his cheek on his chest, and he held him close while he cried.

"Good evening, fellas. Am I interrupting anything?" Nadine Bassette asked as she approached Ned and Billy. The madam, realizing that she was intruding on a moment, started to turn around to leave. "I can come back later."

"Oh no, it's okay," Billy responded, a little embarrassed. "You two talk. I have a little more cleaning to do inside." Billy wiped his eyes, stood, smiled at Nadine, and walked inside.

Taking a seat on the stoop that Billy had just vacated,

Nadine sat her poodle, Rufus, down by her feet and pulled an envelope out of her bra. Handing it to Ned, she said, "Here's Willa's rent from the mayor. You'll see that it makes its way to Claire and Gail, won't you, Hun?"

"I'll do it," Ned replied.

"You're worried about that young man, Ned Wilson, but there is not a thing you can do. Only time is going to heal his wounds. Not that his family has a very good track record in the healing department." Nadine had spent a near lifetime watching her friend, Ruth Blakely, suffer from her emotional scars. "But maybe he'll break the mold."

"I know you're right, Nadine. It's just that he didn't deserve what happened to him."

"We all have to live with the results of things that we didn't deserve, Ned Wilson. You are a kind man, like your daddy was. It's a shame that you don't have his libido, Sugar, I'd wear you out."

"You're a kind woman yourself, Lady," Ned replied, shaking his head in something less than a full laugh at Nadine.

"Why shucks, Sir. I'm just an old whore with a soft heart."

"Ha. I'd suggest that you be on your way now before you get us both in trouble."

Nadine rose from the stoop, kissed Ned Wilson on the top of his head, patted his shoulder, and said, "You might want to put on a jacket, Sugar, you're shivering." Looking down at the concrete, Rufus was snoozing, Dewie licking his head, "Let's go, Rufus." Then, the madam disappeared into the South Georgia night, wiping sweat from her brow with a cotton handkerchief. The evening was far too warm for anyone to be shivering.

At the same moment, a figure in jeans and a dark jacket, using a house key for leverage, made a long gash through the pink paint of the convertible Cadillac parked on the street in front of the diner.

Out in the county, Wade Hansard, now known as the Noeware Man, was still in hiding. He had been growing increasingly impatient for a return to his text message. Giving in to a rage that had grown insurmountable, he dialed a number and spoke into the recording, an action that he was warned never to do.

# CHAPTER 14
# OWEN'S CREEK APARTMENTS, TENNYSON COUNTY

Nurse Rhonda Conner had had an incredibly long and draining work shift. Her day began at Tennyson General Hospital at 5 a.m. and ended at 2 p.m. She wasn't originally scheduled for a morning shift, but she had been called in when another nurse had called out ill. She left the hospital in time to check on Mama Jo Blakely, a private healthcare job that she had picked up in hopes of paying off her student loans faster. Most days, she wondered if assisting Mrs. Blakely was worth the hassle. She kept a spreadsheet showing the long-term dollar value of each minute spent with Mama Jo in terms of interest saved, which kept her partly motivated. The rest was made up of the suspicion that Mama Jo had worked her way through all the at-home nurses in Tennyson County, and she wasn't sure the Blakely's would find another. Not that Mama Jo wouldn't have deserved every bit of being left all alone. But Rhonda had grown very fond of Cora and had gotten to know her at least well enough to know that Cora's plate of troubles was already plenty full.

After leaving "The Honey Hole," Rhonda went back to the hospital, had a quick late lunch in the cafeteria, and worked another shift—this time, the one she was scheduled for. Pure willpower alone, which Rhonda Conner had cultivated in spades over her three decades of life, had kept her going today until the charge nurse asked her if she wanted to head out early, given that the night had been slow. Now, she was dead on her feet, with thoughts of her cool sheets on her mind as she turned the key in her front door and flicked on the kitchen light.

The television in the small living room projected a blueish glow across the apartment, a true crime documentary playing. Rhonda's roommate, Patricia Barfield, also a nurse at the hospital, lay sprawled haphazardly across the sofa. There was a glass half full of liquor on the coffee table, and a nearly empty bottle of cheap whiskey next to it. Rhonda watched the television, more out of habit than interest, as she began to straighten the room a little. The program's subject was organized child abduction.

Now, focusing her attention on her roommate, Rhonda shook Patricia's shoulder in a failed attempt to wake her gently. Her second attempt was much less subtle, shaking Patricia and almost relegating the woman to the floor—accidentally, of course. "Patricia, it's time for bed. Help me out a little, please," Rhonda said as she started to lift the other woman from the sofa, one of Patricia's arms draped over her shoulder.

"What's happening?" Patricia slurred towards Rhonda's face, the rancid smell of alcohol and unbrushed teeth hanging in the air like a weather balloon. Rhonda said nothing as she maneuvered them both toward Patricia's bedroom, dodging furniture and clicking on lights as they went. Once in the room, Rhonda allowed Patricia's listless body to fall onto the bed, pulling the covers over her as best she could. She didn't bother to undress her. "If you keep going this way, you could risk your job, you know, Patricia." She didn't expect an answer and didn't receive one.

Rhonda allowed herself to stare for a few moments at her roommate and friend. She had a hard time figuring out what had gotten into the normally very responsible young nurse. Sure, Patricia often indulged in a few glasses of wine here and there, but never really went beyond what most would consider a social drinking level. But she'd never seen Patricia fall down drunk, certainly never on liquor, and not for such an extended period of time as she'd seen for the last 24 hours.

Rhonda smiled affectionately at her friend, seeing the contentment on her face, a welcome change from the tension she'd seen for the past day or so. *What in the world is bothering her,* she wondered to herself, backing away from the bed to leave the room. As she turned, she spotted out of the corner of her eye what looked like a newspaper clipping lying half under the bed, half in the open. As Rhonda bent to pick the piece of paper up, she saw what appeared to be a boot box, lid half removed, under Patricia's bed. It was overflowing with clippings.

Though she knew none of this was her business, she looked over the first clipping that she had seen. It was from this morning's paper, and it reported the arrest of Dr. Don Givens.

Rhonda knew that Patricia worked closely with Dr. Givens, but that didn't really explain why the woman would have cut the article out of the paper. When Rhonda knelt beside the bed to put the clipping with the others in the boot box, her curiosity overcame her, and she pulled a few out to look at them. Article after article from newspapers far and wide, some old, some more recent, all documenting one subject—the life of Dr. Don Givens. Rhonda's palms began to prick with sweat when she discovered a large hunting knife buried under the articles. She didn't quite understand what she was seeing, but it gave her a queasy feeling. She would need to discuss this with someone to get someone else's perspective. Trying not to overreact, Rhonda returned the box to its original place under the bed and allowed the breath that she was holding to escape her lungs. As she sat back on her heels, a gunshot sounded from the living room, causing her to nearly fall over. The documentary. Why had the T.V. been so loud, anyway?

Moving quickly now, Rhonda went to her own bedroom and closed the door. She studied it momentarily, then locked it. She didn't bother to turn the light off, thinking over what she should do next. She'd wait a few more hours, then she'd figure out who to talk to about what she had discovered. Another gunshot was fired on the T.V., causing Rhonda to jump again. With that, she grabbed her cell phone from her pocket and dialed a number from her contacts. She waited as each unanswered ring seemed to take minutes. Finally, Rhonda's supervisor from the hospital answered groggily. She quizzed Rhonda, seeking to understand the nature of the panic in her young nurse's voice, before agreeing to attempt to have Dr. Don Givens call her as soon as possible. Rhonda had to wait less than ten minutes.

"Rhonda? This is Dr. Givens. What exactly is going on here? It's the middle of the night, and I have not had the best day."

The nurse explained to Don Givens, the recent state of her roommate, in addition to the contents of the box that she had just discovered under Patricia's bed. The doctor's reaction was one of immediate shock and disbelief. He agreed that Rhonda had done the right thing by letting him know right away what she had found, assured her that there was no need to apologize for calling so late, and let her know that he would get to the bottom of the situation first thing the next morning. He ended the call.

There would be two members of Tennyson County's healthcare community lying awake until sunrise this morning.

## MEANWHILE - GRAND HOTEL, NOEWARE, GA.

Gail Wilson was working late into the night at the front desk when a familiar tap came from the employee entrance, doubling as the hotel's back door. Peering through the eyehole to be sure she knew the new arrival; she opened the door wide. The old woman, face sagging and her clothes wrinkled, pulled her small luggage cart and suitcase behind her as she entered the area behind the desk.

"Well, good evening, Miss Willa. Have a busy day?" Gail asked.

"Oh yes," Miss Willa responded, making her way back to the managerial bedroom suite that she had called home for years. "I had a lovely adventure today, but I didn't see my little girl. Have you seen her?" Miss Willa looked hopeful as she glanced back at Gail.

"I'm afraid not, Miss Willa, but I will keep an eye out for you."

Gail got back to work at her desktop computer as Willa Banks turned in for the evening. Gail had been worried about Miss Willa's living arrangements ever since she had heard that the hotel had been sold. She hoped that the new owners would be as understanding as the former owners were.

Approaching the front desk from the opposite side, Ned Wilson, envelope in hand, greeted his ex-wife. "Good evening, beautiful."

"You'll want to have your vision checked first thing, Ned Wilson," Gail replied with a weary smile. "I've been going over these books for the better part of two hours. I am exhausted."

Handing the envelope to Gail, Ned said, "Here's Willa's rent. Maybe you should finish up your work in the morning and go home and get some rest. Tomorrow is going to be a big day."

After she took the payment, Gail reluctantly agreed, "Maybe you're right. Daddy probably wouldn't appreciate me yawning through the most important political speech that he has ever given, even if I have heard him rehearse it a thousand times by now."

"Yes, but this time, it is for real. Come on. I'll walk you to your car."

Gail Wilson said goodnight to Daisy Wei, who was on the overnight desk shift this evening before she grabbed her purse and met Ned in the lobby. They exited the hotel, hand in hand, as Daisy watched. Daisy smiled and shook her head, wondering how long it would take her boss to come to her senses and return to the man that she was obviously head over heels for.

As Ned and Gail disappeared beyond the hotel's front door, Daisy opened a file document that she had hidden on the computer's desktop. It would certainly be counter to her continued employment if the file was discovered, but so far, she had been lucky. Alone now, she got to work on her side project. It was okay with her that everyone thought she was flighty and computer-challenged; the truth was, she had no trouble with computers at all. That is just what everyone assumed when she had to abruptly minimize her file as others approached the desk so that she wouldn't be caught. There was only one person's opinion that mattered, and she was determined to eventually get his attention. THAT was the reason for the file's very existence. She only had to keep it a secret for a little longer.

# CHAPTER 15
# MIDDLE GEORGIA HOSPITAL,
## 1996

Dr. Jerri Hansard sat in an uncomfortable aqua colored fiberglass chair in the waiting room outside of the Middle Georgia Hospital Labor and Delivery Unit. The hour was approaching 2 a.m. and she had consumed so much coffee that her hands and knees were trembling. Her heart was racing from an overload of adrenaline.

Dr. Hansard was a reluctant part-time member of the staff at the Middle Georgia Psychiatric Hospital, previously known as the Georgia State Asylum. She had taken the position to supplement her income. Her dream was to build a private practice in her home of Columbus, Georgia. She earned decent money as a practicing clinical psychiatrist, but her loans had been significant. Based on her projections, without the additional income provided by MGPH, it would be 15 years before she could pay off her loans and open a practice. With the second job, she figured she could do it in 7. But her training had not entirely prepared her for what she would encounter at the hospital.

The institution, of course, had a reputation. Those with a prurient bent took an interest in the institution's history of experimenting with lobotomies and electric shock therapies, though they were hardly the only institution to have used those methods when they were seen as the next great hope for suffering patients. But the MGPH had been around since the Civil War and, in its wake, had become a locus of nefarious and scientifically dubious research on the psychiatric differences between the races. Overcrowding and a tendency for communities nearby to commit those among them who were more contentious than unwell contributed to the deplorable conditions in the institution. The hospital had been, and continued to be, a place people disappeared into.

Most local residents knew something about this history based on rumor and lore; but few were aware of how little had truly changed at the institution. The nature of the atrocities had changed slightly but atrocities there were. Too many residents were lost or abandoned by their families, many of whom had to choose their struggles. This left residents vulnerable to every kind of mistreatment. The staff who were truly committed to their care generally outnumbered the bad apples, but the latter had come to expect a certain degree of impunity, and they generally got it. Jerri had observed this situation from very early in her tenure, but being so low on the tenure totem pole, there was not much she could do. Sure, she had spoken up anytime she saw unethical or even illegal activities taking place. But what options did she have? She had tried complaining to her shift supervisors and to department heads, who received the complaints with bland thanks for bringing the issues to their attention; nothing seemed to come of it. She could complain to the state medical board, but she had witnessed the desserts of that for other doctors who had tried it. It was, apparently, a career-ender. This though, tonight's situation, this was Jerri Hansard's final straw.

Jerri sighed. If she'd known what she was taking on when she agreed to this job, she might have reconsidered it. It was meant to be just a job. Jerri had her hands full as it was, with two jobs and trying to do her best for her daughter. Tina was a seemingly happy, well-adjusted girl, a good student, and a kind child. She got some benefits from the state to assist with her visual impairment, access to tools to help her use a computer, books in braille, and even a state-of-the-art voice-to-recognition program (though it wasn't very good). It all helped, but it took time to research and help Tina use it. Between this and two jobs, Jerri had too much on her plate to get caught up in the travails of any patient, not even the hidden pregnancy of a state hospital patient who was giving birth at this very moment—yet here she was. She sighed again and checked her watch for the 20th time that hour.

A nearby elevator dinged, announcing the arrival of a newcomer to the floor. The first other person to arrive in nearly an hour. Jerri Hansard stood as a dark-skinned woman with thick glasses made her way out into the lobby, assisted by a metal walker. The black woman looked around expectantly, before laying eyes on her old friend. Jerri met her outside the elevator door, embraced her, and stood back to give her a once over.

"Jesus Christ, you've gotten old," Jerri said to Ruth Blakely.

"Old? Why, I'm currently training for a half marathon. Who are you calling old?"

Jerri laughed at Ruth's sarcasm, but the light moment was short-lived. "Oh, Rue, I have no idea what I have gotten myself into this time."

"You said that you were previously unfamiliar with this particular patient, right?" Ruth asked. She had a knack for getting down to brass tacks.

"Right. Male and female patients are kept separate from each other in the wards at the state hospital. It doesn't bear thinking about who could have done this to her. Honestly, if I had known about this before, I would have spoken up to someone, consequences be damned." Jerri's voice rose with a combination of anger and a growing sense of panic.

"I know, Jerri, let's try to remain calm. Also, let's move over to the chairs, these hospital floors aren't the easiest on my hips."

Once the women were seated, Jerri retrieved them each a fresh cup of coffee. "So, who brought you down from Atlanta?"

"A young man from back home drove me. He was already in Atlanta visiting friends. Luckily, he's good company, as it's quite a journey from the city to here, as you well know. He has taken it upon himself to find a couple of hotel rooms for us. I am assuming that we'll be here for a while."

Nodding in agreement, Jerri asked, "I can't thank you enough for coming, Rue. I didn't know who else to call." She shrugged slightly. "Plus, well, I knew I would need a bulldog for this case. How's Atlanta Legal Aid treating you, anyway? Are you still working around the clock?"

"Yes, I'm still working a ridiculous number of hours, but not nearly as many as I had become accustomed to. They seem to like to pile the bulk of the load onto the baby lawyers right out of school. I'm still putting in far too many hours, but they've eased up on me a bit now that we have a new cohort of babies coming in."

"Well, thank God for small blessings, I suppose," Jerri said somewhat weakly. They'd be there for a while, and she had been looking forward to catching up with her old friend, but her attention was stuck on the patient in the delivery room.

During the lull, a doctor in scrubs approached, his mask hanging from his left ear, allowing his face to be visible.

"Dr. Hansard?" he asked, looking at Jerri.

Standing, Jerri replied, "Yes, I'm Dr. Hansard."

"Dr. Hansard, I'm Glen Phillips. I wanted to let you know what's going on in there. The patient was highly aggravated. In fact, she became inconsolable to the point of extreme distress, so we had to make a decision. It is never our preference to do so, but we felt it necessary to sedate the patient. Shortly, we will be performing a C-section.

"Oh. Is that a safe thing to do? Sedating a woman in labor, I mean?"

"It's not the most common practice, but it's certainly not unheard of. We have done it a few times before."

Taking in the conversation, Ruth interrupted firmly, "Do what you need to do, Doctor; we'll be here when and if you need us."

Dr. Phillips nodded his agreement and, without another

word, went to scrub back up and rejoin his colleagues in the delivery room.

Jerri returned to her seat next to Ruth and nervously stared straight ahead. Ruth, sensing her friend's anxiety, returned her silence but took her hand reassuringly.

Later that early morning, Dr. Phillips once again joined the ladies in the waiting room. The exhaustion was clearly displayed on all three of their faces.

"Ladies, it's a boy."

"Oh, thank God. And Jane, is she okay? The baby, is he healthy?" Jerri Hansard asked. Jane was not the patient's given name, but she had been labeled, along with countless other patients at the state hospital, Jane Doe for lack of knowing a true identity.

"I am happy to say that it appears that both mother and son are going to be just fine," Dr. Phillips replied. "I do need to note that her face and body show signs of severe trauma, though. However, none of it seems recent."

Both women sighed with relief. Later, they were allowed to visit the patient known as Jane in a recovery room.

Ruth glanced at the still-sedated woman. She looked like she had spent eight rounds in a boxing ring with Rocky Balboa. Her hair was tangled in an oily rat's nest and damp with sweat. Her face reminded Ruth of spaghetti and meatballs, lumps and scars filling nearly every surface. "My God, did MGPH do this to this woman?"

"My understanding is she arrived this way, but who knows for sure? But the way they had her hidden away, I can't say that I trust anything that I am told by the hospital staff anymore."

Both of the woman's cheeks and at least one side of her jaw appeared to have been previously broken, causing her face to sag like a deflated balloon. A large lump on her nose suggested that it had also taken a beating—undoubtedly many. Ruth didn't think that the woman's own mother would recognize her in this state. Ruth steeled herself against the thought of what she must have been through.

Ruth and Jerri sat quietly for over an hour, as the woman known as Jane Doe slept. After a while, the patient slowly started to stir. Opening her eyes, she appeared too weak to show the aggression that Dr. Phillips had described. Still, Jerri Hansard thought it best to let the hospital staff know that the woman was coming out of sedation.

A few hours later, Jane Doe's rest was interrupted by what could only be described as a kind of half-waking trance. She mumbled a single word over and over—a word not unfamiliar to Ruth Blakely. Staring at the woman in shock but not completely believing what she had heard, Ruth addressed Jerri Hansard, "Jerri, why am I here?"

"Huh? I told you I didn't know who to call?"

"Yes, yes, you did. But why am I here?" Ruth questioned again.

With a heavy sigh, knowing that her answer was likely to make her sound crazy, Jerri replied, "Rue, you know that I don't believe in coincidences, right?"

"Say it, Jerri, it's been a long night."

"The bible beside Jane's bed over there, it was kept at the nurse's station at MGPH. Despite the labor pains that she was experiencing, she panicked about it being left behind. She didn't want to lose it." Jerri grabbed the bible from the nightstand and handed it to Ruth.

Ruth, losing patience, said, "It's a generic bible, for God's sake, Jerri. What's the issue?"

"It certainly appears to be a generic bible, but there's something different about it." She reached over to the book in Ruth Blakely's hands and opened the front cover.

Jane's repeated word reverberating in her head like an audio strobe light, Ruth insisted, "Jerri—"

But then she saw clearly what Jerri wanted to show her. The book looked like any other bible; the kind distributed among hotels. It had a white vinyl cover embossed with gold. But in this one, the first chapters had been removed, such that it opened with the Book of Ruth.

Ruth Blakely lost no time going to the nurse's station, though she was still radiating astonishment. She asked politely to speak with Dr. Phillips. When the women behind the desk assured her they would certainly be able to help her and there was no need to bother the busy doctor, the veneer of politeness vanished. "We would like to speak with him immediately. So, unless he is presently catching a baby, I'll thank you to fetch him for us."

"You wanted to see me, ladies?" Dr. Phillips asked as he entered the room. The nurses had told him he was about to have his hands full, though this would turn out to be insufficient preparation for dealing with Ruth Blakely.

"Dr. Phillips, it appears that the patient, though admitted under the name Jane Doe, is actually a Miss Wilhelmina Banks from Noeware, Georgia. We'll be taking her back home with us this morning," Jerri said.

"That may be the case, but I'm afraid that without a court order declaring you the legal guardians of Ms. Banks, the state of Georgia would see this as kidnapping," the doctor replied cheerfully, in an informative rather than accusatory way.

Looking over to her friend, Ruth said, "Don't worry, Jerri, we know a guy. I can assure you; Willa will go back to that hospital over my dead body." Pulling her flip phone out of her purse and using her walker to assist her into the hallway, Ruth placed a call. "Duncan? This is Ruth. Why yes, I know very well how early it is, and you know that I wouldn't be calling at all if this weren't an emergency. I'm going to need a favor in the form of a court order for emergency guardianship. Yes, I know how highly unusual that is. Jerri Hansard and I are at the Middle Georgia Hospital with an abused patient. Let me give you the specifics—"

Reentering the hospital room, Ruth let Jerri know that Judge Duncan Boyd was working on her request. Jerri, who knew Duncan as well as Ruth did, still had reservations.

"Rue, there is no way that the hospital is just going to let us take Wilhelmina out of here without a fight."

"Wanna bet? Do you think that the state of Georgia is going to want to argue with an attorney about guardianship of a state mental patient, who was obviously raped while in its care, became pregnant by either another patient or, worse, a member of its staff and then had her condition hidden, rather than being allowed to receive treatment from the doctors on duty to see that she received adequate prenatal care? Oh, and by the way, she has been missing from her hometown for over two decades and would garner more publicity than anyone else in the state of Georgia if they tried to mess with me."

"I see your point," Jerri responded.

"I'm telling you, Willa Banks and her baby are leaving this hospital with us, Jerri. I will not take no for an answer—from anyone."

# PART TWO

The Day of the Campaign Announcement

# CHAPTER 16
# RUTH BLAKELY'S CONDOMINIUM, NOEWARE, GA
PRESENT DAY

R
uthie …
　　Twofer …
　　　　Let me braid your hair …
Ruthie …
I think you could ride a cloud straight to heaven …
Twofer …
Dyke …
Darkie lover …
Twofer …
Ruthie …
Run, Olivia …
Two men ran. One after Olivia. One to get help. A third grabbed Ruth, while Ruth grabbed a rock …
Wooooooooot

. . .

Ruth Blakely gasped as she shot straight upright in her bed, her nightgown clinging to her sweat-soaked skin. Another nightmare haunted her dreams, another night where rest escaped her. Reaching toward her nightstand, she searched clumsily for her glasses. She was legally blind without them. They were sat atop a half-read copy of the Sadie Lewis novel Return of the R.O.G. Applying the thick spectacles to her face, she drew back her bed sheets, threw her legs over the side of her bed, wincing at the ever-present pain in her hips, and stepped into her slippers. Standing with the help of her walker, she grabbed her robe and put it on.

Walking into her kitchen, the mayor could smell fresh coffee brewing. Harrison had insisted on giving her a high-end coffee machine, which she suspected was mostly for his own use on days when he had stayed over. Spoiled, she thought. She had called it "the contraption" but had grown to appreciate its many features – primarily the programmable timer. She reached into a cabinet to grab a cup and made her way toward the coffee maker. She jumped and nearly dropped the mug, thankfully still empty, when her friend Jerri Hansard greeted her with a bright, "Good morning, Rue."

"Jesus, Jerri, you about scared me to death. I suppose that I am not used to having anyone here in the morning when I first wake up."

"Sorry about that. I'm surprised that you got any sleep whatsoever. After all these years, you're still having those nightmares, aren't you?"

"They come and they go," Ruth sighed as she filled her cup with a steaming brew. "Would you like a cup of coffee?"

"Oh, no, thank you. I think I'll grab a cup at the coffee shop downstairs before I head over to Tina's apartment."

"I'd advise you to skip the Mean Bean and get a cup at the diner. For the life of me, I don't see how that place stays in business, the coffee is terrible."

"Noted. I'll be out of your hair after today. I am going to check on Tina, then Meg Givens and I are going to head out to retrieve a rental car for Allison Edwards."

"Well," Ruth said, surprised, "that's very noble of the two of you."

"It's selfish, is what it is. I need to get the hell out of here for the day. It'll be good to clear my head."

"I can see that. Are you doing okay? Holding up?"

"I think that I'm doing as well as can be expected," Jerri replied. "Tina isn't doing well, Ruth. I think she is having a hard time justifying in her head that her brother could be capable of killing someone. I'd like to say the same, but I honestly can't say that I'm sure, though you're the only one I'd be prepared to admit that to."

"Wade Hansard is not her brother. He is her foster brother. They aren't related at all."

"No, technically, you're right, but I raised them both. They grew up under the same roof. Whether or not they were close is beside the point. They were raised as siblings."

"I've actually been thinking about Tina's emotional state, and I think that I have an idea of something that would help as far as work goes."

"Is that right?" Jerri said hopefully. Tina was an eager and extremely bright young woman, but it had been hard for her to find jobs that were willing to accommodate her visual impairment. Not in so many words, of course, nothing that would violate the letter of the A.D.A. But it was already a competitive job market. Her education had been in marketing, and perhaps if she had lived in Atlanta, she'd have found more opportunity, but that would have entailed living far away from Jerri, and neither of the two was quite ready for that kind of distance. "What are you thinking?"

"Well, next year is an election year. There are rules that prevent candidates from running campaign-related business through the city offices. I think it would be great for her to run my reelection campaign but to do so from home."

"Hmm, that's a thought," Jerri replied. "I want you to be careful, though, Rue." She paused for a moment. "Do you remember what you told me when Tina was born? We had just been told that she was blind, and the condition was likely permanent?"

"I told you that you'd be doing her no favors by coddling her. To set the same expectations of her that you'd have for any other child."

"Exactly. So, I am asking, are you coddling her now with this offer?"

"That's what you really think I'm doing? I am not going to ask her to run my campaign because I don't have faith that she could get another job, Jerri. I'm going to offer her the position before someone else offers her a better one."

"I see. But what would you do about an assistant at city hall?"

"I actually have someone in mind, God help me."

## CHAPTER 17
## DRISKILL'S HARDWARE, TENNYSON COUNTY

"Good morning, buddy," Jeremiah Waddell said with a huge grin on his face as he greeted his boss, Tug Driskill. Holding a coffee cup in his left hand, he sat it down to retrieve his work apron. This morning, he was on top of the world, having landed a legitimate job, something that he might actually be good at.

"Jeremiah, come on back to my office real quick. Let's have a chat," Tug said as he made his way toward the back of the store.

Following Tug to his office, Jeremiah's face fell. Jeremiah began to get a familiar feeling. Anytime he thought he had found a job that would work for him, it was all but guaranteed something would happen. As if he were psychic, his gut told him exactly what was about to happen.

"Jeremiah, we've been friends for a long time, haven't we?"

"Yes, Tug, we sure have. Being as we are, I'd appreciate it if you wouldn't string this out if you're trying to give me some bad news."

"I'm afraid that I am going to have to, Jeremiah. I'm a small businessman with a lot to lose, and I am being pressured not to allow you on my payroll. Powerfully pressured."

"Shit! This just ain't fair. Every time I find somebody willing to give me a chance, that bitch—"

"I really am sorry, Jeremiah. I really think you would have been an asset to my business."

"It ain't your fault, Tug. I know exactly what is going on here. Ruth Blakely lives to make my life a living hell."

Jeremiah Waddell stood and removed his apron, draping it over the chair that he had been sitting in, and said, "Well, if you do ever find things have changed, you'll let me know?" Tug nodded, albeit somewhat noncommittally, and Jeremiah left the hardware store. As soon as he was out of eyesight, Tug Driskill picked up the phone on his desk and dialed a number.

"I don't like it, but I just let him go. I don't understand it, but I did exactly as you said."

"Great," replied Cash Waddell before ending the call and placing his phone back into his pocket. He had plans, big plans, and they didn't include his father working outside of their home.

## MEANWHILE, JUST A FEW DOORS DOWN FROM THE HARDWARE STORE ... NADINE BASSETTE'S BOARDING HOUSE, TENNYSON COUNTY, GA.

Nadine Bassette, wearing a blouse that barely covered her ample bosom, was finishing up a phone call. "Just let him know that everything is all set per usual, and we look forward to seeing him this afternoon. His regular girl will be here."

Looking down at the floor, a white poodle barked once, "I hear you, Rufus, but you've already had your breakfast. Want to go outside for a little walk before things get busy around here?"

Just then, the madam's phone rang, and she grabbed it on the first ring, "Ruthie, Sugar, what can I do for you on this fine morning? Ummmm, do you really think that is such a good idea? Well, of course, I will drive you."

Nadine could think of about a thousand things that she would rather be doing than taking Ruth Blakely for her first visit in years to see Mama Jo. However, Ruth was one of her oldest friends, and if she needed her, she'd be there.

Now, in Nadine's convertible pink Cadillac ...

"I appreciate you picking me up behind the building, but that was hardly necessary, Nadine," Ruth Blakely said, already dreading the condition that her hair would be in by the time the ladies reached their destination. "Everyone in town already knows about our friendship. I don't think that attempting to hide it now will work."

"Horseshit!" Nadine Bassette exclaimed. "You have to run for reelection next year, and it won't be me who throws a wrench in that plan."

Ruth sat up straight, squinting as the light morning breeze blew dust in her eyes. She watched as the buildings that formed her town gave way to county structures.

Looking straight ahead, her pink hair staying impeccably in place thanks to a near pint of hairspray, Nadine continued,

"What put a bee in your bonnet to go visit Mama Jo, anyway?"

"Harrison called this morning. Apparently, mama is up to her old tricks now that Jessica's death is front-page news, and Harrison's senate announcement is imminent."

"Ah, I see. She's trying to cash in on her silence?"

"That she is. Also, it appears that the other county commissioners have filed a rather ill-timed ethics complaint against Harrison, accusing him of public intoxication."

"Well, he can hardly plead innocent to those charges."

"No, he certainly can't."

"Well, I don't want you or Harrison to give another thought to any ethics complaint. I'll clear that up real quick," Nadine said. "What we have here is just a bunch of limp-dicked county commissioners with their panties in a wad. Trust me, I can attest to both the erectile dysfunction as well as the undergarments. Most of them have been my guests a time or two over the past few decades. I'll just let them know that I'll stay quiet if they will, too. The case will be closed before it's entirely opened, Sugar."

Ruth laughed nervously, knowing that the madam meant every word she had just said, even if it seemed in jest.

# CHAPTER 18
# CRABAPPLE LANE, TENNYSON COUNTY

Nadine Bassette's pink Cadillac, Imogene, came to a screeching halt in the dirt and gravel driveway of Mama Jo's house. Ruth was the first out of the car, reaching toward the backseat to retrieve her folded walker. She made her way to the driver's side of the car, watching Nadine apply a layer of ruby red lipstick while looking at her reflection in the rearview mirror.

"Wow, that's quite a scratch," Ruth said, noticing a long key mark down the side of Imogene for the first time.

"Yes, it is," Nadine responded angrily, "I'll have to deal with that this afternoon."

"Oh, do you have an appointment at the body shop with Wanda? I'm sure she can buff it right out."

"Ha, that's not quite what I meant," she replied as she moved the mirror back into place and exited the car herself. "Wanda will be tending to her next week."

The two women made their way up to the front door of

the small house, Nadine careful not to offer assistance to her friend, a gesture that had been declined too many times to count. Without knocking, Ruth opened the door and entered first, her old friend right behind her.

Glancing away from her T.V. set, which was blaring at a ridiculous volume in order to be heard over Tennyson County's leading Christian music radio station, Mama Jo removed her oxygen mask and spat, "And behold a woman comes to meet him, dressed as a harlot and cunning of heart. Proverbs 7:10." Looking more closely at the women, she continued, "But come here, you sons of a sorceress, offspring of an adulterer and a prostitute. Isaiah 57:3."

Nadine Bassette, blushing a little under her caked-on makeup, said, "I told you this was a bad idea. I'll just go wait in the car." Very few people could make Nadine Bassette feel embarrassed by her profession, but Mama Jo was one of them. It must have been from habit alone because Nadine felt neither shame nor compunction about her line of work but having grown up under the watchful eye of her dear friend's mother, she couldn't quite shake the feeling of shame in Mama Jo's presence. It must have been a form of muscle memory.

Mama Jo yelled in response, looking Ruth over from head to toe before gazing directly into Nadine's eyes, "I wasn't talking to you, whore."

The madam froze in place, preferring to stay close to the front door. She didn't expect that this would be a long visit. She still wondered why they were there at all.

Approaching the hospital bed that her mother seemed confined to, Ruth sat in a chair next to it. Taking the T.V. remote in her hand, she lowered the volume, though Mama Jo protested. "That second verse you quoted doesn't exactly have the meaning that I think you meant it to, mama," Ruth said, "but reading comprehension was never your strong suit, was it?"

"Is there a point to you two Jezebels being here, or have you just come to insult me in my own home?"

"Actually, there is a point to us being here," Ruth answered, "and I will get right to it." She made eye contact with her mother, though Mama Jo turned her head. "Commissioner Tennyson let me know this morning that you made an attempt to blackmail him, and not for the first time, regarding Jessica Walters' murder. He will be giving you nothing, or so help me, I will no longer give you anything. I have done my level best to keep you as comfortable as possible, though only God knows why I feel obligated. Do not contact Harrison again, or you will be cut off. Entirely and for good."

Mama Jo, eyes wide in surprise, both from her oldest daughter's words, as well as her impromptu visit itself, replied, "Get out of my house, the both of you. Do not come back. You disgust me. That boy was an abomination, dressing in lady's clothes. He was born out of a bond of evil. In a more holy country, they'd a stoned him to death."

With a heavy sigh, Ruth stood, using her walker for leverage, "I've said all that I plan to."

Heading towards the door, she walked by Nadine and outside, yelling over her shoulder, "The remote is on your nightstand. You may continue to destroy your hearing now."

Saying to Ruth, as she closed the door behind her friend, "I'll be right behind you, Sugar." The madam took her place in the chair that Ruth had just vacated and stared down at Mama Jo. The time had come to face her demons.

"Now, let me tell you something that's been on my mind for years, Hon."

Mama Jo opened her mouth to interrupt.

"Umm, no," Nadine continued, "I'm speaking now." She took a deep breath, then—

"You've spent a lifetime memorizing a book that you don't have the capacity to understand. You look down on me because of my relationships with men, but your man only appreciated you when he saw you reflected in his rearview mirror. You were always more interested in your welfare check than you were in the welfare of your own children. You are pathetic. In fact, you disgust me. You've always disgusted me, you holier-than-thou, hypocritical piece of street litter. That lady out in my car is worth 10 of you, and until you do right by her, I'd get used to the smell of smoldering embers—since you've spent a lifetime on a high horse claiming to be free of sin but engaging in every deplorable kind of exploitation, of your family and everyone around you. I understand that you may not have long left, and that is a blessing—for Ruth, for Cora, hell, for all of Tennyson County. When you finally do take an eternal dirt nap, I want you to remember to do one thing for me: tell Lucifer that Nadine Bassette said howdy and that he still has an unpaid balance at my front desk."

The madam stood and walked out of the house, having slid the T.V. remote just out of reach of Mama Jo. She walked and mumbled, "You nasty rancid skank."

Behind the wheel of Imogene, Nadine cranked the Cadillac with a flourish—feeling liberated. The radio blasted

The Commodores' "Brick House" at an elevated volume. Putting the car into drive, Nadine hit the gas pedal hard, leaving only a cloud of dirt impeding the view of the sticker on the car's bumper that read, "Be Kind ... Always", while Ruth looked at her wondering—but not asking—what she'd been saying to Mama Jo.

# CHAPTER 19
# MIDDLE OF NOEWARE DINER, NOEWARE, GA

Carl and Cora Washington sat in a booth close to the door of the diner. The noise from the breakfast rush impelled them to talk at a higher volume. Carl always insisted that he have a table in the center of the action rather than a quieter corner booth, as the newspaper editor didn't want to miss any of the small town's action. But the consequences of this—especially as his age had been advancing—was frequently needing to ask others to repeat themselves.

Carl took a sip of coffee from his cup and sat it down on the table. He fidgeted with his silverware, avoiding eye contact with his wife as he said, "I've got to cover the proposal for that new stop sign out by Frog Rock this afternoon. There's a new librarian that I need to profile, and of course, Commissioner Tennyson's senate campaign launch is this evening. Not to mention, I have to figure out where to add that A.P. piece about that banker who died over in Albany. I need to clone myself, or I won't be able to get this all done."

"Can't, never could, Carl," Cora replied. "Quit your bellyaching and get out there and show Tennyson County that you aren't quite ready to be put out to pasture. What's newsworthy about a small-town banker's death anyway? Do they suspect some shady business?"

"Indeed, they do, but I don't mean in his death. Well, it could be that as well. The authorities found evidence on his laptop that he was messing with some of the local children."

"You don't mean—?"

"I sure do," Carl replied, shaking his head.

"My heavenly days, what is this world coming to? Well, I have all the faith in the world that you'll work it all out, Carl."

"I'm not a superhero, Cora."

"I know you, honey. You may not be a superhero, but you've always been my hero." Just then, Cora's cell phone rang in her purse. Pulling it out, she read the screen. "It's the school, I hope everything is alright." Answering the phone, Cora maintained a concerned look. "This is Cora Washington. Yes. Thank you. Well, just spit it out then. DRUGS? Are you sure? What kind of drugs?" Carl, wide-eyed and now concerned himself, listened intently. "Uh-huh. I see. I'll tan his hide. That's just a figure of speech. Just to be on the safe side, Principal Collins, I wouldn't get between me and my grandson this afternoon; you might get a knot yanked in your tail, too."

Carl and Cora exited the diner after leaving enough cash on their table to cover their breakfast and a tip. They flew by Ruth Blakely with barely a word, as the mayor entered. Ruth looked at Ned Wilson behind the counter with a confused look, and the diner owner replied with a shrug.

"Carl and Cora sure were in a rush," Ruth said as she reached the counter.

"I have no idea what all that was about," Ned said. In truth, he'd overheard a bit of what they'd said, given that Cora had been practically shouting by the end of the conversation. But he certainly didn't know enough to relate information without getting key facts wrong. Ned was a man you could trust not to gossip. An important trait in the man running the main diner in town. "Having your usual, Ruth?"

"Just coffee, please. I've been out to see Mama Jo. It has put me off of food."

"Here you are, ma'am. I hope the day gets better for you."

"Thank you, Edward. You have a servant's heart, just like your father," she responded, smiling.

"I can't think of a better compliment, Mayor Blakely," Ned replied with a wink.

As Ruth turned her walker around to exit the diner, she stood face-to-face with Chief Ernie Thomas.

"Ah, Mayor Blakely, I was hoping that I'd run into you this morning."

"Well, lucky you, Ernie, you almost did."

The police chief continued quietly, walking beside Ruth as she continued toward the door. "It occurred to me, in all the hoopla last night in your office, that you never told us who Jessica's father is."

"Oh, did I not?" she replied before yelling over her shoulder, "Thanks again for the coffee, Ned. It's so much better than the muddy water they serve across the street." Ruth Blakely left without another word.

## MEANWHILE, IN A CORNER BOOTH ...

Allison Edwards was joined by Dennis Hernandez.

"Good morning, Allison. I appreciate your willingness to see me."

"Well, I think that we have both suffered a trauma, and I'm not sure that my being at your throat is going to help the matter at all."

"Thank you."

Allison continued, "What do you want from me, Dennis?"

"I hate to ask this, but do you happen to know if Jessica had a will?"

"Apparently, Dennis, I didn't know that Jessica had a lot of things. She paused, recalling that she had only moments ago committed to being kinder to Dennis, and continued in a somewhat softer tone. "No, we never talked about a will."

At that moment, Allison realized that reporters were snapping pictures of her and Dennis through the diner windows. She could just visualize the tabloid headlines now, proclaiming that the two of them were having some sort of sordid affair. At that moment, she decided that she no longer cared what the press thought and she was tired of running from them. "I've spoken to the Walters. They are making arrangements for a memorial service in Atlanta for Jess."

"Oh," Dennis replied, "I haven't let myself get that far. I hope you'll keep me posted."

"Under the circumstances, I find it highly inappropriate that you attend."

"She was my wife, Allison."

"So you say, Dennis. However, neither Jessica's parents nor

I knew anything about you. In fact, I'm wondering if this would be a good time to inquire about your evidence of the marriage. I feel it would be the minimum you'd be willing to offer under the circumstances."

Crestfallen, Dennis Hansard stood and replied, "I suppose you're right." With tears in his eyes, he exited the diner.

Allison's phone rang, the screen reading: Mother.

"Hello, Mother, how's Alpharetta? I see," Allison listened, feigning interest. "To be honest, I haven't given my newspaper story any further thought. What I really want to do is just get the hell out of here. I expect that is exactly what I'll do when the F.B.I. releases me to go." Allison ended the call, her exasperation visible, and stood up, but her exit was impeded by Dr. Don Givens standing in her path talking into his phone.

"Well, if Dr. Hansard is out of town, who is seeing her patients?" Don asked. "Who is Dr. Wagner? Well, I need to see him—today." Ending his call and turning to the diner at large, Don asked loudly, "Has anyone seen my wife?"

Allison responded, "She went to pick up a rental car for me. She'll be back this afternoon."

"For you? What the hell? How exactly does she plan to drive two cars home alone?"

"She's not alone," Allison replied, "Dr. Hansard went with her."

Don Givens's face fell and turned bright red at the same moment.

## OUTSIDE THE DINER ...

Nadine Bassette yelled as she walked up the sidewalk, "Cash Waddell, I've been looking for you, Sugar."

Turning in the opposite direction, Cash replied, "I've got things to do, whore, I don't have time for this."

Stopping directly in front of Cash, blocking his exit, Nadine responded, "You know, Cash, I always thought you were a massive dick." With that, the madam looked intensely into Cash's eyes. With her right hand, she found her target, the crotch of his jeans, grabbed Cash Waddell by the bulge in his pants, and twisted with the force of someone trying to turn a stuck doorknob.

Cash collapsed to his knees, tears forming in his eyes.

"Ahh, how disappointing, Sugar," Nadine continued, "I'd call that mediocre at best." She continued down the sidewalk, straightening her blouse. Over her shoulder, she yelled, "Keep your hands and your keys off of my car." She disappeared around a corner, her deep red stilettos clicking on the pavement as passersby giggled at the scene.

# CHAPTER 20
# OUTSIDE NOEWARE ELEMENTARY SCHOOL

Jeremiah Waddell passed a bench facing the elementary school playground. It was occupied by Willa Banks. The woman watched him intently. Noticing her stare, the old man averted his eyes, causing Willa to bow her head in shame. Jeremiah sped up as he passed in an evident attempt to avoid her. After he was out of sight, a thin woman took a seat next to Willa. They sat together in silence for a few minutes, watching the children play on the other side of the fence. Finally, the younger woman said, "Hello, Miss Willa."

Taking her focus off the children and looking at the other woman, Miss Willa responded, "Hello, Dear." She removed a picture from the bible that was sitting in her lap and showed it to Misti Waddell, "Have you seen my little girl?"

"I'm afraid that I haven't," Misti replied, already very familiar with both the picture and the question, as were most of the citizens of Tennyson County. Misti returned her attention to the playground, her heart beating heavily in her chest. Desperation rising in her for her child.

Little Annie Waddell was still too young to attend school, but the joyous giggles coming from the other children on the playground gave Misti motivation. She was determined to gain custody of her child, a little girl that she had abandoned while chasing a high.

She would have done anything to have been able to take Annie out of the Waddell house when she left it a few years back. But she had been in no condition to raise her child then. There was nothing more important to her at the time than getting a fix. Now she wondered if Annie wouldn't have been better off with her anyway, given how things were in the Waddell house. But she couldn't undo her choices from that time. She could only move forward.

Her father-in-law, Jeremiah Waddell, was a small-time criminal. He made his income dealing in stolen goods. Anything from electronic equipment, to automobiles, were available for sale at the Waddell house, if you could really call it a house. Jeremiah and his son Cash lived in a trailer that was in such bad shape, it had become dangerous. Misti's child was being raised in that very place.

Cash Waddell was a different story than his father. While Jeremiah was certainly a menace to legitimate businesses in the county, his son was downright dangerous. Misti had been on the receiving end of his anger countless times. She'd already been a dabbler in street drugs, but they became her refuge in the face of that implacable brutality. The high offered a temporary reprieve from the hell that was her everyday life, and it was usually enough until the day she overheard an argument between the Waddell men that she was never meant to hear. That was the day that she knew her life depended on getting away from Cash.

As Miss Willa and Misti sat beside each other, watching the children in silence, Carl and Cora Washington rushed into the front door of the school. Misti glanced over at them but was immediately startled by Miss Willa appearing to enter a trance-like state. Over and over, the old woman repeated a single word. Misti put a little distance between herself and Miss Willa on the bench, not really understanding what was happening. However, the trance was over quickly, and Willa was back to her forward gaze.

## JUST ACROSS THE STREET ...

Mayor Ruth Blakely, cell phone in hand, waited for her outgoing call to be answered. "Ruthie," the caller said pleasantly, "it's been a while, my old friend."

"Who are you calling old, you old coot?" Ruth replied with a giggle.

"Ha. I'm feeling every bit as old as I am these days, too. What can I do for you this morning?" Judge Duncan Boyd asked.

"I need a favor, Duncan."

"Name it, Ruth, if I can help, I'll be glad to."

"I need a recommendation for a good family law attorney."

"Family law? You finally ready to adopt?"

"I'm serious, Duncan. This won't be an easy case by any

stretch. I have a mother, a recently recovering addict, attempting to gain custody of her child."

"How recently are we talking?"

"Very, I'm afraid."

"Well, you're right, that won't be easy."

"I wouldn't have bothered you with this if it weren't important."

"I'll see what I can do, Ruth."

"You've never let me down before, Duncan."

"Say, let's get together for lunch sometime, Ruth. It really has been way too long."

"That sounds fine to me, Duncan. Maybe the three of us can grab a bite one evening," Ruth said hopefully.

"Well, you know, getting Sophia out of the house is like pulling teeth, classic introvert."

"Well, then, I'll expect an invitation to the house before the holidays."

"That, my old friend, could certainly be arranged. We'd love to see you."

"That sounds mighty fine, Duncan. Now, please get back to me on that family law attorney."

"You got it, Ruth," Judge Duncan Boyd said before ending the call. His wife's hand touched his shoulder gently.

"Why didn't you tell her, Duncan?" Sophia Boyd asked.

"I don't think a quick business conversation on the phone is the best time to tell one of your oldest friends that you have terminal cancer, do you?" She gave him a narrow-eyed look, affectionate but skeptical, one he'd grown accustomed to over their many years of marriage. "I'll tell her, Soph. Next time."

# CHAPTER 21
# TENNYSON PLACE, TENNYSON COUNTY, GA

Claire Montgomery's car eased slowly up the hill where her family home sat, her older brother, Commissioner Harrison Tennyson, currently its only resident. On a normal day, Claire wouldn't be visiting Harrison at lunchtime. She'd wait until her regular visiting time after work. But today was anything but normal. She had to be sure that her brother was in a condition good enough to participate in his senate campaign launch later in the evening, and the only way to do that was to babysit him for as much of the afternoon as she could.

As Claire parked, she grabbed her ringing phone and glanced at the screen. She hesitated, thinking she would deal with this call after her visit with Harrison, but thought better of it and answered. "What's going on, Cash? I am just about to walk into Tennyson Place."

"Meet me this afternoon at the usual place," Cash replied.

"This is not the afternoon for a rendezvous, Cash. Harry's senate announcement is tonight."

"Well, I've got some pent-up aggression that I need to relieve—no need to keep you long."

"Do you ever think about anything else, Cash Waddell? To be honest, I could probably use the stress relief myself. What time?"

After the phone call ended, Claire knocked hard on the old house's door, assuming that her brother was either upstairs or sleeping off a drunk. To her surprise, Harrison Tennyson answered the door quickly.

"What are you doing here this time of day," he asked his sister.

"I thought it would be a good idea to make sure that you weren't in a stupor. Are you planning to ask me in?"

"Of course, come in. I'm actually completely sober today, Claire, and I plan to remain that way. Contrary to popular opinion, I really do understand how important this evening is—to us all."

"I'm glad to hear that, Harry. I've been very concerned about your behavior lately."

"I've lost a child, Claire. Why is it so hard to understand that I might be shaken up a bit?"

"You've lost a child that you never knew, Harry. Hell, you barely knew anything about her."

"DO NOT DISMISS ME, CLAIRE!" Harrison exclaimed, raising his voice and smacking the door with his bare hand, though not hard enough to be alarming. "I've already heard from Camille this morning. Her helpful suggestion was to 'get over it'." He mocked her tone of voice snidely.

"Well, it's seldom that Camille and I agree on anything at all, but we do agree on this. You have been planning this senate run for years, Harry. Do not drop the ball now, not when the goal is so clearly in sight."

"I don't plan to, Claire. I've just been in mourning."

"Well, this afternoon is a good time to emerge from your mourning period and return your focus to the job at hand. This evening, you will be the presumptive favorite to win the party's nomination for junior senator of Georgia, do not screw this up. I'll be by later to drive you to the hotel for the announcement."

"I plan to drive myself, Claire. I could use the time to clear my head and be ready to give the speech of my career." He said the last part flippantly. Camille and Claire, between the two of them, had reminded him daily that today could make or break his chances. He knew they were right, but he had the impulse to rebel against the constant reminders, as if he could forget.

"Are you sure that you are in any shape to get yourself to the hotel?"

"I am sober, Claire, as I told you, and I won't be drinking before the big announcement."

"Okay, brother of mine, I'll trust that you genuinely mean that."

"You have my word. Trust me, hitting the campaign trail and getting the hell out of Tennyson County is becoming more and more appealing by the minute."

"Your wife will be very happy to hear that, Harry. I think Camille has effectively moved to Washington D.C. already."

"Yes," Harrison replied, "it seems she has. By the way, did you get ahold of Congressman Cunningham?"

"I left him a voicemail this morning, reaffirming our wish for him to take up any campaign-related activity with Camille. I don't think you'll be hearing anything else from him."

"Good. That son of a bitch has had my wife, I think he's gotten enough from me."

"Cool yourself, Harry; the congressman will be standing on stage with you this evening. Let's not have any drama, please."

"Nope, not at all. I intend for tonight to be completely drama-free."

# CHAPTER 22
# I-75 SOUTH, TRUCK STOP

Drs. Jerri Hansard and Meg Givens took a seat at a faux wood topped table at a truck stop on the way back to Noeware. They looked over the food-stained menus that were handed to them by an ancient waitress smelling of stale cigarettes and kitchen grease. The women were equally glad to be out of their vehicles, though for different reasons.

"Christ," Jerri Hansard said, rubbing her lower back, "I think all of the driving that I have done in the last 24 hours is catching up to me."

"What are you moaning about, Grandma, at least you have a working radio to take your mind off of your aches and pains, I have been driving in excruciating silence," Meg teased the older woman. "I've had just about enough of my own company, as well as my own thoughts."

"Well, I suppose that you take what you can get when the press has rented nearly every car in South Georgia, and I think we have your daddy's senate announcement to thank for that."

Meg shook her head, "I can't tell you how happy I am to get this announcement over with. I have been anticipating it for so long, I thought this day would never come."

Jerri cocked an eyebrow at Meg and replied, "You don't exactly seem thrilled by the thought."

"Don't mind me. I suppose that I am just a little anxious about it. Especially about seeing my mother."

"I see," the psychologist responded.

"Don't shrink my head, Doc," Meg said, rolling her eyes.

The waitress returned to the table to take their lunch order. They agreed that salads were probably the best bet in the dingy environment. Within minutes, the waitress returned with two salads, dressing on the side, obviously premade.

"So," Meg asked, moving lettuce around her plate, "how long have you and Ruth Blakely known each other?"

"Oh, we go way back, college, actually. We were roommates. In response to Meg's look of astonishment, Jerri continued, "We had the cutest little apartment in Atlanta. Do you know the Little Five Points neighborhood?"

"Is that the place with the big skull?" Meg didn't hide her incredulity.

"That it is. Of course, back then, there was no skull. In fact, the restaurant that now sports Atlanta's most lengthy list of burgers was an all-vegetarian establishment back then. The neighborhood was already plenty weird by that time, but that is what Ruth and I liked about it."

"I have trouble picturing Ruth as a young college student. What was she like?"

"Rue was a lot of fun. Of course, she's always been very serious, she's wicked smart, and she's been through the wringer. But she knew how to have a good time. She had these gorgeous long braids—"

"You can't be serious? Ruth, with braids? I can't picture that. I suppose that I have trouble seeing her as fun now that you mention it."

"Careful, Meg, Rue Blakely is my very best friend. If you had any inkling—"

"I don't mean to be disrespectful, Jerri. You just have to remember that I have known her only as 'Mayor Blakely' or as 'Ruthless Blakely'."

"Oh yes, 'Ruthless', I had a hand in giving her that nickname," Jerri Hansard responded, laughing. "Are you about ready to hit the road?"

"I suppose that we better. Let me just pay the check and run to the restroom."

"How about you just run to the restroom? I'll take care of the check. We'll call it my way of thanking you for the company today."

"Fair enough," Meg responded reluctantly.

Meg proceeded to the Women's Room and closed and locked the door. She walked over to the first stall, saw that it was missing any form of toilet paper, and glanced at the second and final stall. She dropped her pants and underwear and carefully hovered over the truck stop toilet, careful not to touch the filthy seat. Upon finishing, she flushed and headed to the sink. She rolled her eyes at the disheveled reflection that looked back at her. She turned on the water, washed her hands, rinsed her face, and checked her face again. With a heavy sigh, she peeked down at the sink basin as she took her right index and middle fingers and tickled the back of her throat. Her vomit was small in volume from the lack of food consumed over the past 24 hours, but it was enough to make her pull out a toothbrush and mouthwash in hopes of covering up her indiscretion. She brushed her teeth, gargled, and rinsed the sink.

Meg rejoined Jerri by the front door of the little diner. All smiles, the ladies headed back out to their respective cars. Meg had been told years ago by a therapist that she had hired that she had learned to use her eating and vomiting as a way to gain power over something when she seemed to be generally powerless over everything. That was exactly how she felt currently. She hadn't purged in a very long time and was, herself, a bit surprised to find herself revisiting the practice in the last couple of days. But that didn't stop her from going through with it, even knowing how hard it had been to overcome the habit in her young adulthood. She elected to delve into what that might say about the degree to which she was currently feeling bereft of control in her life.

## CHAPTER 23
# THE G.R.I.T. DEPOT, NOEWARE, GA

Ruth Blakely moved much slower this afternoon than she had in her recent history. Like the weight of the world was strapped to her back. As the depot door closed behind her, she reminded herself that her track record of surviving bad situations so far was 100%. Her walker clicked against the tile floors as she approached her old friend, who she was happy to see was standing at ground level, obviating any need to climb onto a train car. Stopping next to a lobby seat, she sat down next to R.W., who, as always, was working on a painting.

"Ruthie Blakely, I felt sure you'd be by today. I wanted to offer you my condolences."

"Thank you, friend, though I don't think that I have much of a right to accept them."

"Sure, you do, Ruthie. You weren't to know what was to happen if that girl turned up. Now, were you?"

"Wasn't I? Wasn't I really to know? I gave her up to protect her from this place. I had no right to draw her back here. Allison Edwards was right: I am culpable."

"You gave her up, Ruthie because your mama didn't give you a choice. She shipped you off like a Christmas package and all but sold your baby to the Walters."

"Those people were good to me, R.W., very good to me, indeed."

"That they were, Ruthie, that they were. I reckon you could say that, well, the passion that you shared with Harrison years ago perhaps started you on a journey that reshaped your entire life."

"Passion? PASSION? Well, I wouldn't call it passion at all."

"Oh, you wouldn't? The way I see it, you two still have a sort of passion for each other. Hell, your lives stick together like white on rice. When I was a kid, my daddy had this bull, and that bull had a thing for one of his milk cows. No matter how hard Daddy tried to keep those two separated, he'd wake up every morning to them just a-cooing over each other in his pasture. But I digress …

"I certainly hope that you are not comparing me to a milk cow, R.W."

"Well, naw, but the situation ain't a lot different. You can hem and haw all afternoon, suggesting that you don't care a lick for ole Harry Tennyson, but you and I know that's not the truth."

"I don't think that I care much for the direction of this conversation, so I'll change the subject. I came here to discuss Allison Edwards."

"Fine young lady, Allison Edwards."

"Yes, she mentioned that you had words with her."

"That I did. It seemed she was looking for a little clarity on some things, whether she knew she was looking for said clarity or not," R.W. giggled.

"Do you think it wise to have had your little talk with her?"

"I reckon it was necessary, Ruthie."

"She doesn't have a personal connection with this town, R.W. I'd advise you to tread lightly. Her curiosity seems to have no limit."

"Ahh, that's where you're wrong, Ruthie. Just because the young lady doesn't have a personal connection to you doesn't mean that she doesn't have a personal connection to this town. I'll suggest to you exactly what I suggested to Allison when it became apparent that she was developing a little obsession with Willa: YOU are not this town."

"Willa? Explain this obsession she had with Willa."

"Don't you worry yourself, Mayor Blakely. I'm pretty sure that I nipped that in the bud."

Standing, Ruth took hold of the grip handles on her walker and headed back to the depot door. "We absolutely cannot have her nosing around Willa, R.W.," she said over her shoulder as the door closed behind her."

R.W. shook his head at the conversation that had just been completed. It wasn't often that one could accuse Ruth Blakely of stating the obvious, but that is exactly what she had just done. R.W. knew the consequences well of Allison Edwards getting too close to Willa Banks, but he expected that she would soon be preoccupied with additional personal drama of her own and have very little time to worry about anyone else, let alone Miss Willa.

Backing up to observe his painting, he smiled and proclaimed it finished. He signed his initials on the bottom right-hand corner and sat down. Nostalgia struck him like a bolt of summer lightning as he took one more look. Staring back at him was the image of a woman in a family way, standing in the front parlor room of Nadine's Boarding House.

OUTSIDE THE DEPOT, RUTH NODDED A GREETING TO Allison Edwards, who refused to return eye contact but stared at two approaching cars, each driven by a doctor. The cars parked on each side of Allison as Ruth continued on her way. The women got out, greeted Allison, and Meg Givens handed her a set of keys.

"I seriously cannot thank the two of you enough for doing this for me. Now, I'll have a quicker way home when the F.B.I. pronounces me a free woman."

"Think nothing of it," Meg said, "but I am afraid that the only car that they had available has a broken radio. The drive here seemed to take forever in relative silence."

With a laugh, Allison replied, "I don't suppose beggars can be choosers."

Meg and Jerri walked away together as Allison climbed

behind the steering wheel of the rental car. Placing the keys in the ignition, she started the car and was stunned by the blaring music. Confusion set in as she just sat still ... listening.

Kate Bush was singing about a man with a child in his eyes.

*Woooot*

# CHAPTER 24
# BILLY WASHINGTON'S LOFT, NOEWARE, GA

Billy Washington ran to answer the knock on the door of his loft after having thrown on a royal blue silk robe. He was still dripping with water, though he had arranged a towel over the top of his head like an Egyptian head wrap. Throwing the door open with a huge smile, then dropping it into a frown when he saw the anxious look on his friend's face, he said, "What's the matter, G.H.? Get in this house and tell me all about it."

"Billy, this town is starting to give me the heebie-jeebies," Allison replied as she entered the loft and closed the door behind her. "What in the world is wrong with her?" Allison asked, watching Billy's cat Garbo moan loudly and jump repeatedly at nothing in the corner of the room.

"Well, ain't that something? They say small children and animals can see ghosts, G.H., and this building is oldddd. You know there's a good chance somebody died in this loft. You can't throw a turnip in the south without hitting a spot where a body once laid. If they all started floating around, there'd be more ghosts than people around these parts."

Shaking her head and rolling her eyes, Allison replied, "There are no such things as ghosts. I know you don't believe that, Billy Washington."

"Well, I certainly want to believe, especially if the ghost looks like that Patrick Swayze from that movie, Girl, Honey. Yeah, I don't suppose I do believe in ghosts, but witches—"

Allison laughed in spite of herself as Billy walked back to answer a new knock on his door. Talking over his shoulder as he walked, he continued, "Remind me to tell you about Delvenia Montrose."

"Delvenia Montrose? What is a Delvenia Montrose?"

"Well, she's from Brazil. No, Bermuda. That's not right; maybe it's the Bahamas."

"Oh, please," Allison teased.

"That's it, BELIZE! And she ain't nothing but a swamp witch, G.H.," Billy replied.

Allison laughed out loud.

Billy threw open his door. Standing before him were two women dressed in what southern folks call "their Sunday best" clothes. The woman standing closest to Billy said, "We are here to share the good news," as she handed a religious pamphlet to him.

Billy gave the paper a quick glance before handing it back, "Girl, Honey, unless the news is that the good Lord is granting me an extra 30 minutes to get ready for this campaign announcement, it can't be that good. Take care now." He closed the door and turned back to Allison. "We have so much to catch up on, but you are going to have to talk to me while I get ready. By the way, I sure appreciate you inviting me to be your plus one this evening. There is nothing that I like better than drinking fine wine and eating good food paid for by wealthy white people, and better still, if I get to dress up for it!"

Allison laughed as she sat on Billy's brightly colored sofa and watched him head to the bedroom to start getting dressed.

"Now, what did Auntie Ruth have to say to you last night? Tell me everything. I don't want you to skip any details."

Turning suddenly serious, Allison yelled, to be heard through the door and over the television that continued to play an old rerun of Soap. "I'm afraid that I am not ready to talk about that. I thought I might, but I don't think I can yet."

"Well, I get that. Of course I do. When you're ready, I'll be here. You want some privacy? You could call your mama. I'll just close this door."

"My mother is far too self-absorbed to hear me out."

"What about your daddy? I never hear you mention him."

Continuing to yell, as to be heard in the next room, Allison answered, "Well, that's a long story. According to my mother, I was the product of a one-night stand—some trucker from Columbus. When she found out that she was pregnant, he didn't want to know."

"Well, he sounds like a coward to me. Hey, you can borrow my daddy. He's a great listener, and you two seem pretty fond of each other. What about Ned Wilson at the diner? He has stood in a few times as a big brother for me."

Allison was about to reply when Billy interrupted, "G.H., will you please turn that T.V. off? I have had just about enough of these ridiculous sitcoms and their tokenism—the commercials, too. If gay people make up less than ten percent of the population, why do we have to be displayed in every ad on T.V.?"

Shocked, Allison responded, "Billy, representation is important, and what in the world brought that on to begin with?"

"I guess I am just in a tizzy right now. Mama called earlier, and it has me on edge."

"What's wrong? Are Cora and Carl alright?"

"Oh, they're fine but upset. It appears that my nephew, Alex, got caught selling pills at his school."

"Selling pills? That is concerning, but I have no doubt that they have done their very best to take care of the twins while your brother and his wife are away."

"Well, that's the trouble. My brother and sister-in-law have decided that my parents aren't doing a very good job of standing in as parents, so they are on their way back to Georgia."

"I see," Allison said, instantly on edge herself, remembering Billy's confession to her that his brother made him the target of homophobic bullying.

"Anyway, let's change the subject, G.H., did the doctors get your rental car?"

"They did."

"Did Meg tell you why she is wearing that wig? Girl looks like Mata Hari."

Laughing, Allison replied, "Billy Washington, half of the African American women from Atlanta to Alaska are wearing artificial hair, but one Caucasian woman wears a wig—"

"Ahhhh," Billy replied, "get you. The lady does you one favor—"

"She's been really good to me, Billy. That one favor was a real doozie."

"Uh-huh. All I am saying, G.H., is don't mistake a woman's need to escape her current reality for a genuine friendship. You did a favor for her, too, giving her an excuse to spend the day pretending that her husband wasn't taking a walk on the wild side."

Before Allison could defend herself, she heard what sounded like paper sliding beneath the door of the loft. Walking carefully in that direction, she looked quizzically at the religious pamphlet lying just inside the apartment. Picking it up, she noticed a handwritten note on the back cover.

The note read:

Tell Allison to talk to Nadine.

Eva

"Billy," Allison yelled, "Who in the hell is Eva?"

# CHAPTER 25
# MEMORIAL GARDENS CEMETERY, NOEWARE, GA

Ned Wilson, wearing his finest suit, which was also his only suit, walked up the paved pathway that led through Noeware's most well-kept cemetery. There were only two others, not counting the one near the Honey Hole that was bulldozed years back to make way for what is now a Dollar General, but nobody likes to talk about that one. He looked around and took notice of the lovely floral displays that adorned each grave. Carol Wei made a point to always have a large selection of the very best artificial flower arrangements available at her floral shop. In the distance, Ned saw exactly what he expected to see: his ex-wife, Gail Wilson, kneeling beside his father's gravestone.

As he approached, careful to clear his throat ahead of time as not to startle her, he was reminded of exactly why and how much he loved this woman. This evening, she looked sensational, dressed for her father's senate campaign announcement. Now, standing next to Gail, he said, "I thought I'd find you here. You better get up from there, you'll get your dress dirty, and we don't want to be late for the party."

Without removing her focus from the headstone, Gail said, "Ned, do you really think he knew how much I loved him?"

"Gail, you were my daddy's favorite person—period. Now, let's get a move on."

"I intended to bring some new flowers today, but the florist was closed."

Surprised, Ned replied, "Closed on a weekday? That's strange. I hope nothing's wrong. That shop is never closed."

"I thought it was strange, too. I hope Carol is okay, especially while Joe is away."

"Where is Joe, anyway? He didn't mention to me that he was planning on taking any trips."

Nodding, Gail responded, "Daisy has been vague about the trip. I got the sense it was a surprise to her, too."

"I'll make a mental note to check on Carol tomorrow morning after the breakfast rush. Now, let's go, woman," Ned teased.

## MEANWHILE, AT NADINE'S BOARDING HOUSE ...

Nadine Bassette watched as her most important client exited through the backdoor in his wheelchair. She counted the substantial stack of cash that he had paid with and made a notation in her business ledger, a ledger that was still kept by hand on paper. She fanned herself with the bills before dropping them into a permanently installed safe behind the front desk. Pulling out a bottle of water from a small refrigerator next to the safe, she wiped the significant condensation across her equally significant cleavage.

"Damn heat," she said as she noticed one of her girls exiting the room that her VIP customer had just left. "Well, Hon, how'd it go?"

"I'd have to say that today was typical," the woman responded as she retrieved a bag from behind the desk that contained a change of clothes.

"Well, Sugar, you've got the easiest trick in South Georgia. The man is paralyzed from the waist down."

"It seems like such a waste of money on his part. I dress up, I sway, I strip, he talks, I listen."

"And the idiot seems to be too racist to realize that Geishas are part of Japanese culture, not Chinese culture."

"Actually," Carol Wei replied, "there is a rich history of geishas in Chinese culture, too. We just call them Gejis." With that, she returned to the room that she had just vacated to change out of the costume that she was wearing and wash the makeup from her face.

Well, Nadine thought to herself, you learn something new every day. Suddenly, the madam raised an eyebrow and walked to the back door. She opened it and looked both ways, positive that she had heard footsteps on the stoop. She shook her head and laughed to herself. Apparently, she wasn't immune to the Noeware Man paranoia. Though, she was sure that she had heard someone there.

# CHAPTER 26
# THE SPEAK EASY MOTEL, TENNYSON COUNTY

Their cars arrived almost simultaneously in parking spaces that were overgrown with weeds emerging from cracks in the asphalt. For obvious reasons, they always parked behind the motel, their cars shielded from the view of passersby on the highway. Cash always made the arrangements to rent a room, having no real status or reputation to protect. Claire arrived precisely on time, and never loitered outside the room for long. She would never be able to explain being in Cash Waddell's company, not at the motel—not anywhere.

Meeting Cash next to the motel room door, she nervously waited for him to disengage the lock so that they would be safely out of sight. As he turned the doorknob, Cash began to kiss Claire's neck softly, almost lovingly. This was new. It was different. She didn't like it. She pulled away, looking back at him with skepticism, unsure why he would be willing to take a chance that they'd be seen, especially now. With a thump, the door opened, having swelled within its frame due to the Georgia humidity, and a gust of stale, overly conditioned air rushed toward them.

"After you," Cash said, stretching his arm out and bowing, the way one might allow a princess to enter before him, all but saying "m' lady." Claire accepted the invitation to enter first and immediately flipped the room's light switch into the "on" position. Gazing across the room's filthy carpet, her eyes met a pair of black Manolo Blahnik heels. Raising her eyes, a pair of flared Carolina Herrera pants covered the legs of the last woman she expected to see in this room.

"Good afternoon, Claire," her sister-in-law, Camille Tennyson, said, seated in a chair, a silk Tiffany handkerchief providing a protective layer between the grimy upholstery and her $1200 slacks. The woman was facing Claire, one leg crossed over the other, her perfectly manicured nails visible at the ends of her crossed arms. "Fancy running into you here, Love."

Claire rounded on Cash Waddell. "You've set me up, you white trash son of a bitch."

"Hmmmmm," Camille interjected, "You know what they say about lyin' down with dogs, Darlin'."

"Hey," Cash said, mocking offense.

Without displacing her stare for even a second from Claire Montgomery, Camille suggested that the woman take a seat. Claire refused the offer.

"Why don't we cut the shit, and you both explain to me what I am doing here."

"Such language coming from a lady, tsk tsk," Camille replied, "but then I don't suppose a real lady would contract the murder of her brother's child." Camille turned her gaze to her nails, admiring them in brief silence.

"I have no idea what you're talking about," Claire responded nervously.

"Oh please, Claire, Cash, and I have been in contact for weeks about your plans. I've been aware of every step of your strategy. I have to say, you've impressed me."

Claire looked as if she might vomit any second. Her face was completely devoid of color, unable to completely process what was happening. "I don't—"

"Oh, Claire, you don't what? You don't understand? Perhaps I can help you out. You hired a white supremacist, whom Cash found in a social media group, to carry out not one but two acts of violence in order to prevent your brother's senate campaign from having to explain any embarrassing faux pas. Faux pas such as siring a mixed-race transgender girl wouldn't play well with the fine folk of rural Georgia. Is that helping to bring any clarity to the situation?" Camille asked as she clicked her immaculate nails against each other in a way that made Claire stare at them while she listened.

*Click Click*

Claire swallowed hard, and she said slowly, "I did no such thing—"

"Oh Claire, you may tamp down the performance. You are among friends," Camille replied with a laugh. "The liberals over at The Academy of Arts and Sciences won't be analyzing this scene for any awards. The dramatics are unnecessary."

"But I didn't concoct any of this. The entire plan, both plans, were Cash's idea. He suggested every detail," Claire responded desperately. Reality suddenly hit Claire like a ton of bricks, "But he was only relaying your plans, wasn't he? Jesus Christ, how have I been so stupid?"

"Behold, the power of suggestion," Camille said, laughing. "But it only works if one is susceptible. You, sister-in-law, proved to be very open to suggestion. Using that nazi to scare the hell out of Don in the alley was an idea Cash had in hopes of keeping the good doctor from getting arrested and embarrassing Meg and the campaign. A lot of good that did, as keeping things in his trousers doesn't seem to be his strong suit. But, when that racist randomly chose Billy Washington to assault, that was just delicious—a twofer, if you will. I'm sure Ruth is still stinging from her favorite nephew's unfortunate little beating."

Cash laughed as Camille continued, "It's just a pity that Don was too stupid to heed the warning. He's a brilliant surgeon, but he's also an absolute sexual deviant." Camille straightened her blouse and looked around the room. Bringing her stare back to Claire, she added, "Speaking of deviants, nice job on the tranny."

*Click Click*

"This is all too much. I don't intend to sit here and listen to any more of this fantasy that the two of you have dreamed up," Claire replied.

"I don't think you are going anywhere, Claire Montgomery. This conversation is just getting started. It's been so long since we've seen each other. We have a lot of catching up to do. Cash, Darlin', why don't you play that voicemail for Claire?"

Cash removed the burner cell from his pocket, holding it

up and activating the speaker function. Looking directly at Claire, he played the message ...

"Harrison, this is Wade. Tell that bitch Claire that I want my money, and I want it now. I did the jobs—I won't be jerked around."

Claire turned a shade of white normally reserved for the dead as the extent of her sister-in-law's premeditated scheme sunk in. She had allowed herself to be manipulated completely by a couple of psychopaths. "You ... you set up Harrison? Your own husband, my brother, to take the fall for all of this? I don't understand. It would destroy his life. Why would you do that? Just to prevent word of his child from becoming public? You are insane! You are both fucking INSANE!"

"My goodness," Camille said, smiling and shaking her head, "there's that language again. I happen to know you were raised with a better vocabulary than that, Darlin'. No, dear, it's certainly not Harrison I'm setting up. The murder weapon has been hidden at your place. You should really invest in a better security system. One anonymous call to the police, and they'll have all the evidence that they need to put you away."

"My God," Claire said, "that's why the security camera was covered at the end of the hotel's security footage. Cash. You went back for the knife."

Cash nodded, showing his teeth with the accomplished smile of a dog who's been told he's a good boy.

"I just don't understand. You had so much to lose from this—why would you risk it? You'd be throwing all of your chances away. They all rest on Harry," Claire asked, genuinely confused.

"I wouldn't be throwing anything away, Claire. First, you aren't going to say a word about any of this. Second, if Harrison was arrested for murder, I would be the guest of every news magazine show on television. The world would have sympathy for poor little ole me. I'd be the toast of New York and D.C. society, even if my husband wasn't a senator. These days, folks love nothing more than a true-crime drama told firsthand by an innocent bystander. Next would be the book deal, the talk show, and the product lines. Either way, I come out on top. But of course, the best-case scenario is a winning senate campaign. Harry getting arrested would just be the next-best option."

"Why? Why in the hell would you do all of this?" Claire asked, already knowing the answer.

"Oh Claire, for the same reason that you went through with all of this—to avoid scandal. Our political base is big on traditional Southern family values. It wouldn't do to have an illegitimate bi-racial tranny child and a son-in-law with a hard-on for the same gender associated with our candidate. These unfortunate hurdles would prove to be just a little too much for Harrison to win a Georgia senate primary. I just figured out a solution that would get rid of two of my biggest problems at one time."

"Harrison—"

*Click Click*

"Oh, Claire, my husband is the least of your worries. What will you do when Ruth Blakely discovers you had the only child she'll ever have killed?"

No longer able to support the weight of her body, Claire fell into a sitting position on the bed. She placed her face in both hands and began to weep. Looking up, mascara smeared on her cheeks, she addressed no one in particular, "No one was meant to be killed. That nazi was supposed to scare the life out of Jessica, not end it. He must have completely lost it when she fought him."

"Yes, it seems he did—pity. That doesn't make her any less dead, though, does it, Darlin'? However, you're in luck. I have a way for you to avoid all this drama. It seems that a close friend is in need of a general manager for his hotel. It would be a lateral position, probably not paying much more than you currently make, but certainly more than you'd make in a penitentiary. I'd accept that position if I were you."

"But the Grand Hotel and the campaign need me," Claire replied, tears streaming from her eyes. "How would I explain a sudden departure to the new owners—to Harrison?"

"Claire, I am sure that the new owners of the hotel will recognize that Gail is more than capable of rising to the position of general manager, she's earned it. She's also much younger than you, so they'd have the position filled for many more years," Camille said with glee, "leave Harrison to me."

*Click Click*

Now aware that she had lost this battle, if not the life-long war that she had fought with Camille, Claire asked, "Where is this job opportunity?"

"Denver. And you start next week."

Claire was astonished that Camille had planned every minute detail of this plan. She couldn't believe that she had let herself be played like a marionette puppet by this bitch and her lapdog. "Even if I agreed to go to Denver, how would I explain this to Stan?"

"Now, this part is just fun. No one outside of this room

needs to know any of this. You can confront Stan with the upper hand. Nadine Bassette may be the queen of confidentiality, but a few of her girls don't mind talking. It appears that your husband is a bit of a perv, and apparently, Nadine's Boarding House has a little kink on the menu. Let him know that he goes with you, or you file for a very public divorce. Ask him if he is up for a little brutal humiliation."

Claire exhaled—defeated. "I—"

Camille smiled sympathetically, "Every story needs a villain, Claire—a big bad. I recommend that you accept that Colorado offer before the world assumes that villain is you."

"I have to go get ready for Harrison's announcement."

"You won't be attending the campaign announcement nor serving in any capacity on said campaign. Pack your stuff, Claire, and enjoy the Colorado winter. I imagine you'll need to buy some new outerwear."

Without another word, Claire left the motel room. Surveying her surroundings one last time before addressing Cash, Camille said, "Speaking of the campaign announcement, I need to burn these clothes and shower. I may never get the stench of this place off my skin."

"What about Wade," Cash asked, though he was pretty sure that he already knew the answer.

"Tell J.B. to turn off the security lights and take out the trash," Camille replied, standing and brushing herself off.

"One thing I don't understand—"

"Cash, Darlin', I have no doubt that there is plenty that you don't understand."

Ignoring the slight, Cash continued, "Why did you tell

Claire that the actual murder wasn't supposed to happen when you told me specifically not to let Jessica leave the room alive?"

"You've done your part, Cash. Leave everything else to me," Camille Tennyson replied.

Cash Waddell exited the motel room, closing the door behind him. Camille Tennyson pulled her cell phone out of her Louis Vuitton purse. She pressed a number in her contacts, labeled simply as C.B. After a few rings, a woman answered. Disguising her voice, Camille said, "Craig Burton, please." The call was transferred to the appropriate line, and a man answered.

"This is Craig Burton."

"It's Camille. It is all taken care of, just as you asked."

"Excellent, my dear. Excellent."

## CHAPTER 27
## FOOD FOR THOUGHT
## MEAN BEAN COFFEE,
## NOEWARE, GA.

Cora Washington thanked the barista as he handed her a decaf latte, then made her way to a table already occupied by her husband, Carl Washington. "Honey, are you sure you don't want anything?" she asked.

"I'm sure. Ruth is right, the coffee here is terrible. I can't believe you are drinking that stuff."

"I just wanted something warm, and with the diner closed due to everybody going to Harrison Tennyson's campaign announcement …"

"Yes, the worst kept secret in the state of Georgia. What's troubling you, Cora?"

"Who says there's something troubling me?"

"Woman, you and I have been married for so many years; I know when you are going to sneeze about five minutes before you do it."

"If I'm honest, I am worried about Calton Jr. heading home. Do you think we failed the twins, Carl?"

"Well, now, if providing for their every need is failing them, then I suppose we have failed miserably."

"Carlton obviously thinks we failed them, or he wouldn't be rushing back home to save the day."

"You talk as if you won't be happy to see our son, Cora. I think he'll be alright once he gets here and sees for himself that the kids are in good shape."

"And Billy? Will he be in good shape once his brother returns home?"

"What is that supposed to mean?"

Cora avoided direct eye contact with her husband as she replied, "I mean, Noeware is not a very big town, and it certainly isn't big enough for both of our children to be here at the same time—it never was."

Carl allowed himself a deep sigh. Though he wanted to pretend otherwise, he knew his wife had a point, and truth be told, he was just as concerned.

At a corner table, Dr. Don Givens joined nurse Patricia Barfield, who had already ordered two cups of coffee in anticipation of his arrival. "Patricia, I appreciate you finding an out-of-the-way table. This hasn't been the easiest few days."

"No problem, I just appreciate you meeting me. I know you must have a lot on your plate right now, as well as a few questions. I'm hoping that I can clear a few things up for you."

Don took a sip of coffee, grimaced at its bitterness, and asked, "I certainly do have a lot going on, not the least of which is what Rhonda Conner told me she found in your bedroom. I hope you can clear that up. But I am not going to lie, it has me very concerned."

"I'm sorry that Rhonda felt the need to alert you about this rather than ask me about it. I thought as my friend—"

"Well, she did alert me, so I would appreciate an explanation. I am all ears, as they say."

Patricia took a deep breath before beginning her explanation. "Well, it's true that I have followed your career for years. I've collected every article that I could find. I'd hoped to get to know you without alarming you."

"I see," Dr. Don Givens replied, "and how is that working out for you?"

"I never thought you'd find out about the articles."

"I'm afraid you've lost me. You've collected articles documenting my entire life. You've taken a position at the hospital in my department, where we work closely day in and day out. You've befriended my wife and me. You've even agreed to be a surrogate for us." Don looked around the room, realizing that his voice was escalating.

"Yes, that was a mistake."

"Which part was a mistake? Because I am having a hard time determining if you are an obsessed sociopath or just a wanna-be fangirl."

"Look, I know how it looks, but I am not a nut. I'm—"

"You're what? Spit it out before I decide that a restraining order is warranted."

Tearing up, Patricia blurted, "I'm your sister!"

Don froze as if someone had pressed some cosmic "pause" button on the remote control of his life. He didn't know what he'd expected to hear from his coworker, but this hadn't been on the list of possibilities. His other mental pre-written responses were suddenly useless. All he could say was, "What the—?"

"It's true, Dr. Givens, Don—"

Don felt as if every ounce of blood in his body had drained out. Every hair on every surface was standing on end. He fought the urge to vomit, his gut souring on the bad coffee. He kept his face expressionless, though, something he'd practiced as a surgeon. Never show outward alarm. "I honestly don't know what to say."

"I'm sure. I am so sorry; I had no intention of you finding out this way. You see, I am not a crazy person. I am a proud person. I never had siblings growing up, so when I realized that I had an older brother—"

"I can't comprehend this."

"Oh God, you did know that you were adopted, right?"

"Of course. I have always known that my parents weren't my birthparents, but—"

Patricia pulled several pictures out of her purse. She placed them on the table in front of Don Givens, who stared at them silently. "It's true, we are half-siblings. We don't share a mother, but here are a few pictures of our father."

Focusing on the top picture without touching it, Don said the first thing that came to mind. "Is that Frog Rock?"

"It is," Patricia replied. "That car he is leaning against was his pride and joy, or so Mother says. It was a 1970 Chevy Nova."

Without looking up, his eyes remaining on the man in the photograph, Don said, "You had agreed to be our surrogate. What about the knife Rhonda saw?"

"I did agree to be your surrogate, and that was a complete mistake. I let this whole situation get out of hand. Obviously, we were going to have to have this conversation at some point because I couldn't carry a baby for you. The level of deception grew bigger and bigger, and the story became out of control. I didn't know how to tell you all of this, how to come clean without making you hate me." Patricia stopped talking, realizing that panic was setting in, and her speech had accelerated. Taking a deep breath while lowering her voice, she added, "The knife belonged to our dad. I thought it would be more appropriate for you to have it."

"The truth is, I have no idea how to feel right now. I think I better go." Don stood to leave, forcing his currently weak knees to perform their intended function and move him toward the coffee shop door.

Patricia, giving in to her emotions, allowed the tears that had been welling up to flow freely down her cheeks as she watched her brother leave the shop. A caring hand touched her shoulder as Cora Washington sat beside her. "Are you okay, Sweetheart?" Cora asked.

"Not right now, I'm not," Patricia replied, reaching for the photos, the most prominent of which featured the light blue Chevy Nova that had once transported Olivia Tennyson in its trunk, driven by one Craig Burton.

## MAIN STREET

Mayor Ruth Blakely exited the building that she called home. The sun was just beginning to set over South Georgia, and the streetlights were slowly beginning to glow. As she started to turn around, she jumped as a hand made its way to her shoulder. "You just couldn't leave it well enough alone, could you?" Jeremiah Waddell asked as Ruth turned to face him, keeping her walker between her and the man.

"As is often the case, Mr. Waddell, I haven't the slightest idea what you are talking about, and I'd thank you kindly to take your last remaining hand off of me."

Jeremiah cleared his throat and removed his hand, "My new job at the hardware store, my first day was also my last. You know, you like to give me hell for what you reckon I do for money, but you use your power in this county to keep me from getting any other kind of work. You can't have things both ways, Ruth."

"You are a parasite, Jeremiah Waddell, you and that son of yours. Nothing would give me more pleasure than to see you both rot in prison, but I would settle for seeing you both achieve legitimate employment. This may come as a shock to you, but I had nothing to do with you losing your job."

"One day, Ruth Blakely, I am going to have enough of your bullshit," he said as he continued down the street. Ruth yelled behind him—

"You mean the way you had enough of Mary? You'll answer to God one day for what you did to my friend, Jeremiah Waddell, and I suspect you'll steam like a clam in the pits of hell for it."

"Well, is that any way for a lady to speak on Main Street?" Jerri Hansard asked with a laugh as she approached Ruth from behind.

"That son of a bitch."

Jerri placed a calming arm around Ruth's shoulder while

concealing a sheet of paper behind her back, "Rue, you know he isn't worth it."

Shaking her head as if to symbolically clear her mind, Ruth asked, "What exactly is keeping you in Columbus, Jerri? It's certainly not a wife and kids. The latter lives here; the former is non-existent."

Smiling at her closest friend's bluntness, Jerri replied, "Thanks for the reminder, Rue. Now, you know that I have a practice in Columbus with patients who depend on me."

"Yes, you certainly do. However, you also have a practice partner who could assume your patient load. You have people here who love and need you, too. Besides, there is plenty of crazy in Tennyson County. You'll be thriving here in no time."

"Speaking of crazy," Jerri said as she handed Ruth the flyer she was holding, "you might want to get to the bottom of this." She gave Ruth a pat on the back and went upstairs for the night.

"Ruth Blakely, just the woman I was looking for," Chief Ernie Thomas yelled as he crossed the street.

"What the hell is this, a parade?" Ruth asked herself as her third visitor in the past 10 minutes approached.

As the chief moved closer, he asked, "Are you ready to tell me who Jessica's father was, Ruth? The FBI is going to press you on this."

"They already have, Ernie, just this afternoon."

"And what did you tell them?"

"The truth, I'm just a 'slut'," she handed the flyer to the chief. "Here, read for yourself."

Ernie Thomas looked at the flyer, which featured a picture of Ruth with the word SLUT printed in all capital letters underneath. He diverted his eyes from the paper to Ruth's eyes, confused about what he was seeing. The mayor lifted her arm to display, as a spokesmodel on a game show might display a prize, that all of Main Street was decorated with flyers: every lamppost, every bench, every building façade, every mailbox, every trashcan. Every available public surface was decorated with a picture of Ruth just above the word SLUT.

Standing in the shadows, just far enough down Main Street as not to be seen by any of the passersby, Dennis Hernandez answered his vibrating cellphone, "This is Agent Hernandez. No, I don't think anyone suspects a thing. Oh, spoiler alert: the mayor is Jessica's mother. I'll keep you posted." Dennis Hernandez ended the call, placed the phone back into the pocket of his pants, and continued his stroll.

*Woooot*

## GRAND HOTEL BALLROOM

Music from the live band blasted throughout the elegantly designed ballroom of the Grand Hotel. Though the acoustics weren't perfect, as the room was not built to be a music venue, the sound was nevertheless good.

♫ I knew a guy who was working the lines
'til he flipped his jeep and broke his spine.
Two months back from a tour of Afghanistan. My Pops told me before he died
'If you enlist, I'll skin your hide.'
And pointed to his prosthetic-filled pants. ♫
Allison Edwards and Billy Washington were standing near

the back, drinks in hand, swaying to the tunes. Allison, finally placing the current song, turned to her friend, "I can't believe that they were able to get CannonandtheBoxes to serve as the warmup band for the campaign announcement."

"Cannon and the who?" Billy asked, attempting to shout over the music.

"CannonandtheBoxes. They are a band out of Athens. I caught a show they played at The Dark Horse Tavern in Atlanta once."

"Athens? That little cutie at the microphone doesn't look Greek to me, G.H., but I'd like to see him on the side of an urn," Billy responded with a smile.

Giggling, Allison added, "I'm starting to finally figure out when you are putting me on. Grecian urn, Keats, very clever."

"Who? Anyway, Athens, Greece or Athens, Georgia, they are a pretty good band either way," Billy replied. "Do you think that singer is looking at me? I'm pretty sure he is looking at me."

"You're ridiculous, and I love you for it," Allison responded, finally able to enjoy herself just a little for the first time in days.

"Don't look now, G.H., but it looks like they are setting up for the big event behind the band."

"It's about time. From what I hear, this announcement has been a very long time coming."

"G.H., I want to thank you again for making me your plus one tonight. I wasn't sure, all things considered, that you'd still be writing your story on the town."

"Well," Allison replied anxiously, reminded again of Jessica and of the last time she saw her alive. Jessica had wished her luck with her story. She'd been so proud of her. "I won't be writing a story on Noeware, after all. But I have agreed to write a biographical story on Commissioner Tennyson."

"I see—" Billy replied, letting the music make up for his lack of knowing what else to say on the subject.

The ballroom filled with applause as CannonandtheBoxes took a bow and left the stage. The key players for the campaign announcement began to take their places.

Looking at the stage, Allison recognized Senator Richardson, the senior U.S. senator from the state of Georgia. She obviously recognized Dr. Meg Givens and her sister Gail Wilson who were standing next to their father, Commissioner Harrison Tennyson. "Billy, is that woman—?"

"Yes, G. H., you are looking at the one and only Camille Tennyson."

"She's stunning,"

"Uh-huh. Don't you dare be fooled, Girl, Honey. You know that song about the devil coming down to Georgia?"

Smiling, Allison replied, "Yes, and—?"

"You are looking at the inspiration. And wait, yep, that devil is wearing Prada."

"You are simply crazy, Billy Washington."

Senator Richardson took to the podium to make a speech that Billy and Allison felt must have taken an hour to give. As he was winding down, he prepared for the all-important introduction. "Ladies and gentlemen, I would like to introduce to you the next senator from the great state of Georgia—Camille Tennyson."

For nearly a minute, one could have heard a pin drop in the ballroom of the Grand Hotel. The crowd was, by turns, still laughing, slow to catch on, or already registering bewilderment. Harrison Tennyson stood perfectly still, only his eyes showing shock and betrayal. Gail and Meg stared straight ahead in disbelief. Camille Tennyson was all smiles.

Then, the room filled with thunderous applause. The attendees gleefully appreciated the apparent surprise that the Tennyson family had pulled off.

Harrison Tennyson looked over at Congressman Cunningham. The congressman shook his hand while whispering in his ear, "I tried to warn you, Harry. Maybe, in the future, you'll take my calls." Harrison pulled back, fighting the urge to faint. He looked at his wife, still trying to convince himself that this was all just a very bad dream.

Camille Tennyson leaned over and embraced her husband. She looked as if she could barely contain her excitement. Slowly, her lips kissed his cheek before moving up to his ear. "Give my best to Ruth, Darlin'," she whispered. "Now, smile for the cameras like a good boy."

Billy and Allison stared at each other as if they had just witnessed a horrific car accident. Finally, Billy said, "Jesus, this is just like that time Cecile on Another World showed up, Sandy—"

# EPILOGUE, NADINE'S BOARDING HOUSE, TENNYSON COUNTY
1996

It took the better part of 36 hours for Judge Duncan Boyd to secure an emergency order allowing Wilhelmina Banks to be released from the hospital and into the custody of Ruth Blakely. The timing was perfect, as Dr. Phillips refused to discharge his patient due to the Caesarean section that was performed until he had been able to observe her for 24 hours. Even then, he was hesitant due to her obvious pain level, but he was convinced upon being assured that she would be taken to a location within only a few miles of a local hospital.

The car containing Ruth Blakely arrived first, pulling behind the whorehouse. Ruth exited quickly, unfolding her walker to stand. A second car, driven by Jerri Hansard, parked beside it. Jerri leaned into the back seat, placed a light blanket over the lap of the infant in a car seat, and then hopped out of her car to face Ruth.

"Rue, I still don't understand why we brought Willa back to Noeware," Jerri said.

"I think it makes sense for her to be surrounded by familiar scenery. Atlanta is too big and too busy for her. You heard the doctor say that she is terrified. Hell, you said she had an episode at the institution."

Jerri nodded in agreement with Ruth, "That she did. But you said that you'd never return to Tennyson County, Rue."

"I did say that, didn't I? Well, perhaps I was always destined to, Jerri."

"Why can't I shake the feeling that we are doing something wrong?" Jerri asked as the backdoor of the boarding house opened, revealing a very pregnant Nadine Bassette.

Nadine walked outside and embraced her old friend, Ruth Blakley, "Well, Sugar, aren't you a sight for sore eyes?"

"It's good to see you, Nadine, this is my friend Jerri Hansard," Ruth replied, returning Nadine's hug. "I certainly appreciate you allowing Willa to stay with you for a while. You are a true lifesaver."

"Think nothing of it. I made up a room, and it's near the kitchen. We don't use it much anyway. I can't imagine that hanging out here in the dark is doing much for Willa's already fragile mental state, and my feet are swelling from all this extra weight. Let's see about getting her inside. I still can't believe that you two were able to arrange to remove her and the baby from the hospital."

"Well, it appears that the lady can be a bit ruthless when pushed," Jerri Hansard replied.

"Ahhh," Nadine said, "Ruthless Ruth Blakely, ha, who knew?"

Ruth walked to the backdoor of the car she arrived in and opened the door to have a word with Willa. She stood up as Jerri approached.

"I suppose that I should go ahead and take the baby back to Columbus with me," Jerri said, reaching into her purse. She pulled out a business card and wrote her home address on the back, dropping a few items onto the gravel pavement in the process. "Nadine, all my information is here on the card. Please, feel free to call me if you need anything."

"I sincerely appreciate your willingness to foster the boy, Jerri," Ruth said.

"What do I call him? It doesn't seem right just to make something up. I have to call him something. What is Willa's father's name?

"Wade, call him Wade," Ruth answered as she opened the car door for Willa to exit. Ruth threw her arms around Jerri Hansard as they said their goodbyes. Willa, noticing the fallen papers from Jerri's purse, bent to pick one up, though the pain of doing so was excruciating.

Jerri's car backed out of the driveway as Ruth assisted Willa into the house. A young Ned Wilson stood from behind the steering wheel of the car that had brought Ruth Blakely back to Tennyson County. He looked at Nadine Bassette as she said, "Ned, Ruth Blakely always had a heart as big as the ocean, but she was never close to Willa Banks back in school."

"Is that so? Well, maybe she just saw an old acquaintance in need—"

"I don't buy it," Nadine responded. "The lady is putting her career, her entire future, at risk to help this woman. This woman that she barely knew."

"Well," Ned replied, "whatever her motivation is, knowing Ruth, we won't know it until she decides to tell us."

"No, maybe we won't, but what I do know is that Wilhelmina Bank's daddy was named Jimbo, not Wade, and if that woman was my sister and dead on a slab, I couldn't identify her with a gun pointing at my head, with all of those breaks and bruises. How do you reckon Ruth knew who she was?"

Nadine glanced suspiciously over at Ruth and Willa, who were making their way into the house. Just as they reached the threshold, Willa lifted the paper that she had retrieved from the ground, a photo, showed it to Ruth, and asked, "Ruthie, have you seen my little girl?"

## UNCLE J.B.'S RESIDENCE, TENNYSON COUNTY

### PRESENT DAY

Cash Waddell entered the barn at the back of J.B.'s property. An impatient Wade Hansard awaited him, ready to make his way out of town. Leaving the barn door slightly ajar, Cash walked past Wade and turned to him, "I've got your money. I told you not to call."

"You ain't been answering my texts, Harrison. What was I supposed to do?"

"You were supposed to wait here until I came back, just like I told you to," Cash replied.

Wade's focus was on Cash Waddell, not the man who had

entered the barn behind him. "Well, let's have it so I can be on my way. I've had enough of that nig—"

Before Wade could finish the word, the sharp handle of a broken pitchfork entered the back of his neck and exited the front of his throat. Blood poured from the wound as if from a faucet, filling every inch of the shirt the nazi was wearing. First, he fell to his knees; then he sprawled on all fours before finally lying face down on the dirt floor—eyes opened wide with shock.

Cash nodded to J.B. as he exited the barn. He was barely halfway across the yard when he was serenaded by the squeals of hungry hogs, making a meal of a young man whose life had both started and finished in a cloud of mystery in Tennyson County, Georgia. The Noeware Man.

## RURAL ROUTE 33, TENNYSON COUNTY, GA.

Rubber galoshes sank into wet muck with every step she took. Her path lit only by the glow of an almost full moon. Stopping next to a fire pit that housed only glimmering red coals, she knelt and placed a small log onto the coals, along with some tinder, which she stoked to a medium flame. Her hair was wrapped in a red bandana. She wore an ankle-length cotton dress with a floral print that seemed to belong to a different era. On a flat rock by the fire, she laid out a single white dove's feather, a dried echinacea bloom, and a lady's watch with a broken clasp.

As the light of the fire illuminated the displayed items, the woman said—

> "When darkness falls
> and the moon is bright,
> the owls hunt,
> the gators fight.
> River creatures emerge
> though they stay out of view.
> The timing is right,
> Ruth, I'm talking to you.
> You may try to run,
> but you cannot hide.
> You'll need to take heed
> of those on your side.
> Though there is upheaval,
> things can turn on a dime.
> Find your way to the swamp, Ruth
> finally, it's time."

The old woman, skin as dark as licorice, placed the items from the rock into a silk bag and placed the bag into her dress pocket. She stood slowly, back aching from advanced age, and made her way back toward her house, spitting a wad of saliva from the pinch of snuff that she held between her cheek and gum. In the swamp that was just past the fire pit, a bullfrog croaked in the night. Air bubbles appeared on the water's surface as an alligator descended into its depths. Pausing at her mailbox before heading to her front door, she made sure that its contents were not important. She closed the box and patted the words on its side, D. Montrose.

*Heh heh heh heh heh*

**To be continued …**
**Woven Branches**
**Book 3**
**The Book of Ruth**

# COMING SOON BY G.L. YANCY

### Woven Branches

### Book 3

### The Noeware Man

All characters and situations in this series are fictional. Any similarities between the characters/events and actual people/events, either living or deceased, are purely coincidental. I made this all up, y'all.

Independent authors live or die by your word of mouth and online reviews. If you enjoyed this novella, please consider leaving a review on Amazon, Goodreads, or wherever you normally review books.

To stay up to date on all things *Woven Branches*, please follow the "G. L. Yancy" and "Woven Branches" Facebook pages. You may also email your full name and email address to glyancybooks@outlook.com to join my mailing list. I will never spam you, only let you know when a new release is available.

I am forever grateful for the opportunity to entertain you ... Please, be good to each other.

# ACKNOWLEDGMENTS

As always, there are many people to thank for bringing a book to life. If I leave anyone out, please know that your contributions were no less important; I am just getting senile—

Thank you, Fay Jordan and John Ross Branch, for answering specific questions for me. Thank you, Tiffany Bowerman, PA-C, for providing healthcare-related information, and Claudia Hamilton of LivingProof Recovery in Rome, Georgia, for answering 12-step related questions. If I got any of these details wrong in the book, the blame falls completely on me.

Thank you, Cannon Rogers of CannonandtheBoxes, for allowing me to use your band in the book. Y'all, CannonandtheBoxes is a real band out of Athens, Georgia, please find their songs wherever you download music. Lyrics featured in this book are from the single, "Abel's Blues".

Thank you, Julie Murphy, Kelly Green, and Jim Ford, for suggesting fun ideas, whether you meant to or not.

Thank you, Brenda Edmonds, Becky Jones, and Debbie Pruitt, for providing a lifetime's worth of material. I hope you three can feel your family's legacy throughout the Woven Branches series. I love you all so much.

Thank you, Angelia Feathers for your beautiful illustrations for social media. Because of your tireless work, fans of Woven Branches are able to meet the folks of Tennyson County long before they ever open a book. I am so appreciative.

Thank you to my dream team: Jennifer Kuzara, Merritt Smith Croland, and Angie Occhipinti. These women edit my books, either creatively or grammatically. As I have said before, they turn this storyteller into a writer, and I can't thank them enough for all that they do. I would truly be lost without them. I love you three more than you will ever know.

Lastly, thank you to my readers. I absolutely love hearing from you all. I adore hearing which characters move you, either in a positive, or not so positive way. I enjoy your plot speculation; I revel in your shock. While Woven Branches is a passion project for me, I write it for you. I am just so grateful that you care, because that is the purpose of art, to make one feel something.

Sending everyone so much love until we meet again—Be good to each other.

If you enjoyed this book, please consider posting a review on Amazon and GoodReads. Positive book reviews are imperative to the success of independent authors. We do not have large publishing houses to promote our work; we have you—and I would bet on all of you any day. Also, please consider joining our email list at glyancybooks@outlook.com. I will never spam you.

Made in the USA
Columbia, SC
15 June 2024